Rosha

Rosha

Vishal Bhandari

Cedar books

Published by:

Cedar books

An Imprint of

Pustak Mahal®

J-3/16, Daryaganj, New Delhi-110002

☎ 23276539, 23272783, 23272784 • *Fax:* 011-23260518

E-mail: info@pustakmahal.com • *Website:* www.pustakmahal.com

Sales Centre

■ 10-B, Netaji Subhash Marg, Daryaganj, New Delhi-110002

☎ 23268292, 23268293, 23279900 • *Fax:* 011-23280567

E-mail: rapidexdelhi@indiatimes.com

■ **Hind Pustak Bhawan**

6686, Khari Baoli, Delhi-110006

☎ 23944314, 23911979

Branches

Bengaluru: ☎ 080-22234025 • *Telefax:* 080-22240209

E-mail: pustak@airtelmail.in • pustak@sancharnet.in

Mumbai: ☎ 022-22010941, 022-22053387

E-mail: rapidex@bom5.vsnl.net.in

Patna: ☎ 0612-3294193 • *Telefax:* 0612-2302719

E-mail: rapidexptn@rediffmail.com

Hyderabad: *Telefax:* 040-24737290

E-mail: pustakmahalhyd@yahoo.co.in

ISBN 978-81-223-1088-7

Edition 2009

Printed at : Param Offsetters, Okhla, New Delhi-110020

To their sacrifice of small joys that have resulted in an unimaginable gain towards my debutante writing, I dedicate this, my first novel to my two wonderful children – Varun & Vibha...

Acknowledgements

Creativity has been my long-time companion, since the time I can remember. She has been my loyal friend who introduced herself to me when I was probably four or five years old. From then on, our companionship has resulted in my learning to paint, beginning to sculpt on my own, and further in time learnt the craft of film making too. Indeed, it has been a long friendship between the two of us, that has stretched over three decades and I hope it lasts a lifetime.

Writing wasn't altogether new to me as writing screenplays had become my practice over the years. However, as it has always been the case with me in the past, where I found certain things could be best captured in a painting and some in a sculpture and the combined juice of all creative forms could form cinema. Just the same way when I desired to share some of my memories, I found writing as the most effective form, for it allowed one the liberty to express oneself wholeheartedly in words.

The daunting task of writing a novel haunted me for years. It was a feat I had to accomplish and it remained to be so until now, when I sit to write down the last but most important pages where I cannot forget to acknowledge all those besides

Creativity, who stood by me with their faith in my capabilities and the confidence that I would manage to accomplish the task I had set myself to.

First, I have to mention the immense contribution and support I received from Mr Arish and Mrs Neena Sahani. When everybody else ridiculed me for my decision to take a plunge into creative arts and pursue it as a profession, these two stood by me. They believed that I could do it. This happened a decade ago and since then there has been no looking back. Five films written and directed by me in three different languages and four international awards to endorse my contribution to the world of international cinema should only encourage me to follow my instincts further.

Vrinda and Talat have been of immense support... my newfound friends who introduced me to a world that is almost alien to the world in which we live. The secret world of men and women that exists but never makes it presence felt was introduced to me by them and that is where I found Rosha. Therefore, without their companionship, writing a novel would have remained to be an unfulfilled desire so far.

Swatantra, just what the name signifies – Freedom. He is a friend who offered me the freedom to pursue writing and forget all other worries for the time being. The immense support that I received from him during those months, when I was engrossed in writing, can never fade from my mind and heart. He is a friend who finds pride in seeing his own friend move forward. Few of his kind exist in today's times and I think I must have done something exemplary to deserve his friendship.

Lastly a mention of my wife – Bharati, not out of formality but because I wanted to express my gratitude to her in a manner befitting the years of love and care she has showered over me. She and I go over two decades of companionship, making her only younger to my eldest friend, Creativity.

So now I take this opportunity to thank her for all the years she has spent with me, never once compelling me to compromise with my goals. Never once has she complained of the limits she had to make do with when finances shrunk to all time low. Not once has she told me to find a more stable means of livelihood. I do not know where she draws her strength from, but I am sure that she has stood strongly through my struggling years, and to this day is by my side. I need to thank her for all that she has sacrificed and all those heart-aching situations she must have battled. Therefore, plainly thanking her would not be enough, so I have waited for a befitting moment and it happens to be the ink of her toil and the paper of my perseverance on which I have managed to pen *Rosha*.

Finally, I would bow down to the understanding and tolerance shown by our children, Varun and Vibha. Over the months, when I have been busy writing, they have sacrificed their countless opportunities of joy granted to them. Invariably, I have heard my son explain to his little sister in a hushed voice, "Papa is writing, he should not be disturbed." Children, I can only thank you for all your support.

Author's Note

The story of Rosha is an incredible blend of beliefs that stands as tall and robust as pillars of faith, morality, integrity, ethics, and over it rests the roof of humanity, under which we the people have learnt to ignore its sanctity and practise the most unthinkable deeds today.

The greatness of thought and the contradiction in practice have left us stranded in a world today, wherein it is very difficult and almost impossible to decide whether we should practise the virtues we were taught to follow, or imitate the majority that thrives on doing the opposite. If survival is the question that one faces, then how much one values one's virtues needs to be weighed. For if to live is what life is all about, then one should carry on and follow and mingle with the herd.

This is a story of a human who fearlessly perished for her beliefs and yet lived on.

A relation between a deportee and an officer that was given the task of doing so can't end up resulting in a subject for a novel; intriguingly it has.

Contents

1

A Rose to Remember

It was a beautiful sunny day in the spring of 2009 when my children decided to participate in a flower show that took place in the city every year. We had grown a few roses which would often catch the eye of any passer-by. Noticing their exquisiteness, a few would surely stop and enquire about where we had purchased the plants from.

They would often find the reply a little unbelievable and probably one filled with attitude. My children would tell them that we had planted rose seeds and nurtured them from there on. The enquiring people would always feel that we had trained our children to never reveal the secret as though. Anyways, the fact of the matter still remains that the roses in our little terrace garden were indeed grown from rose seeds.

As we walked through aisles of various flower arrangements that had filled the atmosphere with a riot of colours and myriad fragrances, I for a moment found it difficult to spot our own flowers in them. My wife and I started looking for our own plants, when our daughter came running towards us with excitement shimmering all over her face.

"Papa our flowers got selected for the 'Best Rose' prize!" At seven years of age, I could not expect my daughter to manage her excitement and English grammar as well. She was delighted about their victory. It was she and my son who had actually nourished the plants, from the time they sprouted out of the seeds. They had looked after them like their little pets; and lo, their perseverance and care had paid off.

We were all very delighted as my daughter guided us to a table, where my son stood proudly alongside our champion rose. When his eyes met mine, he ran to give me a big hug. People looked at us as we celebrated our little victory. A flower from our humble little garden had been adjudged as one of the most beautiful roses in the town.

While we were congratulated for cultivating such unique specie of roses by many, I knew that those accolades would soon be followed by the same question, which we had answered so many times before – "How did you graft such a beautiful breed?" Alternatively, "Which nursery did you purchase the saplings from?" My honest reply, once again, disappointed the little enthusiastic crowd that had gathered around the roses. People assumed that we did not wish to share the secrets and walked away with a polite smile and a mind full of grudge.

All we had done was feed the plant water once a day and till the soil from time to time. For some reasons unknown to us even today, our plants have thrived just on that for so many years, so what else I could have said besides adding a mention of the organic manure that we kept adding into the soil twice a year and the amount of earthworms that kept at work ardently.

Other than that I could have added to my answer was, a mention of the love and attention that my children would give to all our plants. I had indeed kept that part of the answer to myself. To the curious horticulturists, love and attention might not have sounded as tangible additives that could enhance the plant health. Thus, my humble reply seemed nothing more than routine while they expected to learn a new technique of rose cultivation that they were not aware of so far.

Everything aside, our roses were now being photographed by the press, as they were to appear in the newspapers the following day. A press photographer casually enquired about the specie to which our roses belonged to.

"Rosha," I replied.

The photographer made a note of it in his diary and moved on. Actually, I had no knowledge of the species but I could never forget the person who had given me those seeds. So on the spur of the moment, I decided to give our roses her name – Rosha, meaning a blooming rose in Pashto. Indeed, she was true to her name. Rosha was an Afghani girl of twenty-two or so, belonged to an erstwhile aristocratic family of Afghanistan and had given me those rose seeds as a parting gift.

My wife wondered why I had never told her the name of the specie of our roses before. I told her that it was not the real name of the specie, but that of a girl who had given them to me a few months ago. She did not ponder much as she understood that if I had not told her about it so far, then there must surely be a purpose to it. A secret that I was not supposed to reveal and she was not supposed to dig.

That evening, after the flower show, our children insisted for a dinner treat and I obliged. Thus, along with our champion roses we seated ourselves in a restaurant that we usually frequented. While I sipped whisky, my children feasted on their favourite kebabs and my wife relished the soup she had ordered, I kept looking at those roses.

Memories filled my mind with images of Rosha. Her voice began to resound in my ears. That day, flowers named after her were declared to be the most beautiful ones, I am sure if Rosha had the opportunity or the inclination, she herself could have well been adjudged one of the most beautiful women on this earth.

Rosha appeared no less than a budding beauty queen. Similar to the inimitability of the roses, Rosha was a rare combination of simplicity, beauty and wisdom. A glimpse of her could fill any man's mind with various fantasies of spending a lifetime with her. Those who did not feel that ways could rush to a physician for a thorough check-up and advice, and for those who shared the sentiment would agree that she was the one. No man would have wished to take her as a daughter or a sister. Nevertheless, I did, as both. Not that I needed medical advice to reassure myself about my manhood, but then at times, restraint is also a test that manhood needs to undergo. I did. I passed and yet I think I had failed in a way.

I had remained to myself, mostly that evening during dinner, and after that too as I poured another peg for myself at home. My wife had changed into a comfortable caftan and joined me on the couch. She knew for sure that my mind was somewhere else, and did not wish to disturb me by asking any questions in that regard. She just wanted to be beside me. In my profession, secrets remain locked within our memories, in our hearts and files, of whom we are guardians, and which can go to our graves, even if that is what it calls for. My wife was aware of my nature of work, therefore my occasional mood swings did not bother her anymore.

I do not remember when she went to bed or when I drifted into my study and began to pen down my memories of Rosha. A secret should have, by no means, found a way out of me, but for a few reasons I felt very strongly that this secret would only serve its purpose if it were to be made public.

Therefore, in the company of my memories, mounted on the vehicle of words, I travelled to that fateful night which seemed a usual night then, with the usual chill of December and the usual homely banter. Lounging with my glass of whisky, trying to counsel myself on cutting down by a few pegs the least and so on, when I received a call from someone I cannot tell. Not because I did not know who was calling, but because in my line of duty, one is not supposed to tell. I was to be a part of an operation and had to leave for the same right away.

Unpredictability and being ready for any situation at any given time was an assumed quality that any officer of my kind was expected to have. A few minutes later, I was ready and on my way to meet my colleagues at a place I cannot reveal, to learn more about what I was expected to do that night.

❑❑❑

2

The Raid

I arrived at the agreed place at around 8:45 p.m. A few of my colleagues were already there, and we had to wait for a few more to arrive. In our line of work, such kinds of meetings happen in dimly lit bars or restaurants, where people are busy enjoying themselves and the noise levels are too high for anybody to overhear our discussion.

A few minutes later, we went into a briefing about the task on hand as well as each ones individual role in it. It was a simple raid, wherein we needed to smoke out illegal immigrants who had been evading deportation in the past and were absconding too. A fruitful tip had led one of our officers to their new hideout. This time around our department had already acquired necessary paperwork, and approvals needed for their deportation. Otherwise, they would have to be kept in a beggar home until the deportation formalities were complete, which could take from a few days to a few weeks, depending on the nation they were to be deported and the relation of our country with the other.

We were eight of us in all, including four from the police department. All of us were dressed in casuals so that we would not draw anybody's attention when we moved into the area where we were supposed to conduct the raid. I was one of those officers who had not been working on this case, thus none of the suspects could recognise me. Therefore, I was supposed to lead the pack.

My job was to manage a smooth entry into the house and get them to pack and leave as calmly as possible. Just in case things did demand force, other officers were to take their positions and do as briefed once I signalled them. We dispersed to meet once again at the location of the raid, and went about our tasks assuming that all were in their respective positions at the decided time.

On my way to the target, I thought it was the easiest task assigned to me so far, in my career of over a decade and a half. Trust me; I had beaten hard-core criminals out of their wits. My knuckles would derive power purely out of the crime I wanted those bastards to admit. I had earned a reputation for administering such a lethal blow, that my knuckles either would tear into the flesh on the cheekbone of the guilty or would land him a few feet away from the point he was last standing.

On such instances I have always wondered, where did that blow come from? I would glance at my knuckles as though appreciating them for the job well done and carry on with my inhumane treatment. That night, a knock on the door was hardly a task for my knuckles, unless matters took a turn for the worst.

A few minutes later, I was walking into an apartment building that seemed to have decent citizens living there peacefully. Neighbouring children still seemed busy at play, enjoying their Christmas break to the fullest. While the elderly were busy returning home or going about their own work. Nobody had the time or interest to even glance at me a second time as I took the stairs to the second floor. My fists, snug in my suede jacket, I walked up to the door of the house and knocked decently enough. It was met with no response from the other end and this happened twice before I attempted one last time.

An elderly woman, on the wrong side of fifty answered the door on my third attempt. I could see the questions in her eyes, even before I could ask her one. I introduced myself as so and so, from such and such department, and was there to meet one Mr Adnan Peerzadeh. Besides, I also demanded her passport. She kept gazing at me in silence. I could sense that she was terrified. Even if she did not have a grasp on English, she had understood what I had asked for. It is strange just as emotions have a universal language, so does law.

As expected, she did not return with her passport, instead a male, maybe her son, six feet-two, in his late thirties, came straight to me wearing an impressive leather jacket with fur collar. I knew it was Adnan – the man we were looking for, I had seen his photograph during the briefing.

I asked him acting innocent if it was he. Adnan felt relieved as he assumed that I did not recognise him. He told me that in fact he too was waiting for Adnan to return. Adnan had bit the bait I had thrown at him. I gave him one good look and just to ease him out a bit, enquired if I could see his passport in the meanwhile.

While he thought of an excuse, I had finished my mental math on him assuming he were to take a jab at me. "Now I do not expect you to be carrying your passport in your pocket, so go inside, and get it, there is no need to panic, it's just a routine check," I said to Adnan to encourage him, further his belief that I had not recognised him.

The mighty host invited me in and I followed with exactly two steps in, thus giving him no chance of shutting the door behind me. My colleagues could still have me in sight and cover me, just in case. Adnan vanished into the other room for some time. I sensed that he did not have what I was looking for – the permit to live in the country. In short, he was overstaying illegally and I was going to make him homeless once again.

One might wonder what kind of a job is this. Trust me; in our line of work, this could be the easiest task we perform. It is like asking Picasso to paint a canvas in front of a gathering of a thousand people. He would surely paint a horse and enthral the onlookers. Why only a horse? Because he knows it fully and is surer of his horse than himself, and more than anything else, that empty canvas does not stare at him, challenge his imagination, and compel him to think. Similarly kicking out illegal immigrants to us is what painting a horse for Picasso might have been.

Adnan returned a few minutes later with a crisp bundle of thousand rupee notes and handed it over to me with his passport beneath it. I took a good look at the notes. They were real and fifty-thousand rupees in all. For a moment, I wondered what this man was doing here to afford such a heavy bribe. He did not realise that this was his second wrong move.

"Come to the office tomorrow and collect your passport," I said to him taking his passport and the bribe, secured in the breast pocket of my jacket.

"I need the same amount for the rest of the people living with you by tomorrow," I said as I turned around to step out of the house.

That demand of mine took Adnan by surprise. "But officer I thought this was enough for everybody… that is how much I would pay usually," he said.

"Bad luck, the price just went up from the time I joined," I replied as I walked out of the house with Adnan in tow.

"But officer we are just students, please tell me how we can afford to pay so much," asked Adnan.

I looked straight in his eyes and questioned, "Which college does that lady, who opened the door, go to? Which course is she doing?"

Adnan took a patient look in my eyes and I made sure not to blink.

"I am sorry I don't have the amount you desire. So what are you going to do? Throw me out of the house at this hour of the night?" I still did not blink.

The expressions on my face maintained calm. I stepped out a little further into the corridor and lit a cigarette. Adnan did not know that I was lighting the cigarette to signal my colleagues and not because I wanted a smoke badly. Honestly, I was helping my colleagues and myself.

Even Adnan could not have imagined how seven more men like me appeared out of nowhere in an instant and stormed into the house. Adnan was handcuffed and taken away. I handed over the cash and his passport to my senior, and stepped out of the scene as planned. As I stepped downstairs the decibel level in the house kept rising. One could easily hear men arguing, women squealing, utensils falling in that house. However, what surprised me was that none of the neighbours bothered to step out of their houses and check what was going on.

While I waited near my car nursing myself with a generous dose of Dopamine, I wondered how lonely man had rendered himself in the crowded metropolitan cities of the present day. Not a single person seemed to hear all that yelling and noise that was clearly audible to me even at the distance where I stood. Indeed, modern thinking had taught man the technique to isolate himself from anything that did not concern him.

While I did not let myself slip into deep thought on the changing trends of humanity, my colleagues began to bring down the deportees. They were altogether fourteen of them.

We had the exact number of cars waiting to take them to the airport. A few formalities to be done would take us about an hour to complete. We would then transport them to the international airport, a two hour something trip at that hour of the night and back before sunrise.

Probably I would meet my kids while they were on their way to school the next morning. My wife would not ask where I was the whole night. One advantage that comes with my job is that the wife never doubts her husband's loyalty towards her and even if she does, she has to keep her questions to herself as the husband would plainly answer back saying, "I cannot tell."

While I kept looking at the deportees being fingerprinted and while other formalities were underway, one of my colleagues came to me and reported that a girl held a switch knife to her throat and threatened to slit it if anyone dared to touch her. I lost my cool. I raced through the stairway and into the house. Most of them were already seated in the cars meant for them except a girl who refused to leave. She did not mind dying there, but she just did not wish to leave.

When I got past another wailing relative of hers, and moved the thin silk curtain that separated me from having a clearer view of her, I saw the most beautiful face I had ever seen in my whole life. As I mentioned earlier, at the beginning, all that applied to any man who got a glimpse of her.

There she was... shapely, fair, beautiful, untouched, and any incredible expression that professional writers might use to go on defining her in a few pages at the least. Here she was...

speaking chaste English and shifting her sight on each one of us from time to time, warning us that she would jab the knife into her throat if we touched her.

It was slightly a film-like situation, but I was not in a mood to play. I took a good look at her, and then all who surrounded her, and ordered somebody who did not exist, to take her away. Her look shifted in the direction I gave orders. For a split-second, she was off-guard and it was long enough for me to grab the knife with one hand and pin her to the ground with other.

It happened so fast, that even she would not have realised. I maintained pressure on her back, but she was not going to rebel as expected. She had broken into tears. She had tried her last move and failed. She was heartbroken, lost, and had given up.

I released her from my grip asking her, "Are you okay? Can I now expect you to follow me downstairs into the car?" She nodded, signalling a 'Yes'. I helped her stand, asked her to get her stuff as we were already getting late. She looked around the room and grabbed a leather bag.

"Alright then, let's just leave," she said. "I would not need any of my stuff to where you would send me."

I reasoned with her but did not persist. I assumed she might have folks back there and she would be fine or probably she liked travelling light. Little did I realise then, that she was going to leave me a burden of memories, which I would find difficult to dispose off all my life.

❑❑❑

3

The Journey Begins

That was how I first met Rosha. Not exactly a suitable circumstance to meet one of the most beautiful women I had met until then. I escorted her downstairs to where my people had gathered with the rest of the deportees standing in a line. The police took charge of Adnan for various criminal activities he was involved in. He was to remain in a police lock-up for the time being.

As for the rest, my senior allocated the ones we were to accompany to the international airport. As usual, I got the most notorious one in my share. Only difference being that the most notorious of the lot was an exceptionally beautiful girl – Rosha. I could see envy building up in the eyes of my colleagues as they escorted their share of the lot to their respective cars. I accompanied Rosha and another lady, who must have been in her late thirties.

Two constables sat in the back seat while Rosha and the other lady in the middle, and I took the seat next to the driver. Seven cars carrying thirteen deportees and eight of us drove out together. Once our car had gained rhythm, I turned back to look at Rosha. I told you, she had a face that made it very difficult for anyone to keep his eyes off her. Rosha's eyes were moist and seemed like those of a dead woman with a dead stare, looking out of the window. I knew that she was not happy to leave, but so should have been the case with her companion too, and she did not seem as disturbed.

"Why are you so unhappy? Don't you like returning to your country?" I asked Rosha.

She maintained her dead stare, as if analysing my approach and replied a few seconds later, "I don't belong anywhere… I guess."

Her voice was as beautiful as she was but at that moment, it seemed very sombre.

"You speak very good English as compared to the others that belong to your part of the world," I remarked to make the atmosphere a little friendlier for the following two-three hours of the journey.

Rosha turned to look at me, "Oh! So you are impressed with my English."

"Indeed… people from your part of the world don't speak that well, and I have not heard anybody speak without a typical accent," I complimented.

"I was learning it further. In a few years to come you might have known me as a writer, and now…" her tears felt like droplets falling to the ground after the rain had stopped.

Since I had not worked on the case, I knew very little or almost nothing about them, but I could surely sense that Rosha might have been very close to some kind of accomplishment, when we decided to send them back. I was not feeling guilty of what I was doing, but I would be lying if I said that I was not feeling sorry too.

"Look madam, there is no use of weeping now. You should have known that this could happen to you if you did not have the permit to stay."

"You are right, officer. But then there was a time in my life when I did not even have the permit to live, and I survived all these years. I guess that might have made me wishful," she said this looking out of the window as though imagining her life going past swiftly.

"Can't I claim political asylum?" she shot back turning to look at me at such pace as if she had found a way to beat me at my own game. Similar to the way one exclaims 'Check-Mate' making his last move, sure, that his opponent would have to give in.

"I think you could have. But then you were here for a good two years and if I am correct you did not try to explain your situation in that manner. Besides you possess a Saudi passport, what possible political asylum can you claim?"

Rosha's long and shapely fingers gripping the headrest of my seat slipped away with her last hope. She once again turned to gaze out of her window.

Rosha's companion clarified with her broken language skills, "She Saudi not... I Saudi not too... me from Baluchistan... Iran... me... her Afghanistan... Kabul... you know?"

No sooner did I hear that, I thought to myself – how had I even assumed that I was going to have a smooth trip? In so many years of work, I had never had the luxury of resting back and having a peaceful chat with a convict, and with such confessions coming up in less than thirty minutes since our journey commenced, I knew that my task for the day was far from over.

"Is that true madam?" I asked Rosha pointedly.

Her nod signalled her acceptance.

"So how did you get Saudi passports?"

"If you cannot help me... why do you wish to know? Put us on a plane and fulfil your duty to your government," she said gazing out of the window like a wife who answers because she has to and within that answer she hopes that you realise that she is not happy talking to you.

"Listen madam, I need to know that the passports belong to you and that you did not steal it or something or else you would have trouble when you land there."

"The passports belong to us... but we don't belong to that place. And the place we belong to, there is nothing left to return to..." she replied.

It was strange that the women belonged to a different nation and possessed a passport of a different country. I had their passports in my possession, thus browsed through them carefully just to check if they were tampered or something like that. Nothing seemed wrong with the passports but something was surely wrong with the whole case as such.

While I wondered what could be the reason or motive behind all this, the driver steered the car into a rest area and we all stepped out of the car to stretch a bit.

My colleagues got tea for everyone. Rosha had mannerisms in her, she thanked the constable who offered her a cup, but with me, she had no hopes left.

"Is Adnan your brother?" I asked her once again attempting to begin afresh.

She signalled – No.

"So, who is he to you then?" I questioned, slightly puzzled.

To this day I wonder, had I not asked her that question, she would have remained to me just another deportee, who would fade from my memory in time. However, what followed that question has compelled me to store that experience for posterity.

❑❑❑

4

The Story Begins

Curiosity on the professional level and compassion on personal front was driving me closer and closer to Rosha. I just could not find logic in her story. On one hand, she was not hiding the fact that she was an Afghan. On the other hand, she had a Saudi passport. To make matters even more suspicious for herself, she was living with a man like Adnan. All seemed incomprehensible with a woman like Rosha in the middle of it. I wondered if we were being hasty with the deportation exercise. It was not my prerogative to know as it was not my case, but as of then, I had become a part of that case. Therefore, I needed to convince myself that we were doing the right thing rather than regret the hastiness later.

Rosha was not interested to know my motive of persistence, and neither was I going to reveal that to her.

"So does Adnan also come from Afghanistan?" I asked her redrafting my earlier question one more time.

"I am related to him in no way. In fact none of us that you are deporting is related to one another," replied Rosha.

"You mean to say that old lady is not Adnan's mother?"

"Officer, to look like a family one does not need to be blood brothers. If people decide to live in harmony, they are quite capable of doing so. But more than often they only give in to such virtues when all other possible ways of suppressing each other's existence are exhausted."

With her opinions, the bluntness in her words and the way she had so quickly prepared herself for the journey to follow, Rosha seemed more like a convict who was waiting to be taken to the gallows. Beyond a certain point of time, the convict realises that the time has come for him to walk the last mile. Seldom does any convict revolt in those last moments, as they have by then, made peace with themselves.

Unlike in the case of convicts who face gallows after spending at least a decade behind the bars to temper their agony and kill their hopes of returning to the normal world, here was a girl who seemed like just about old enough to begin taking a few steps by herself, and such profound thought...

"How old are you?" I asked her without lacing my question with any kind of cordiality.

Rosha looked at me as if to decide if I was righteous enough to know about her personal life. She maintained the same look and words began to flow out of her, "I turned fourteen on the last day of the last century. As it wound up its affairs of a millennium, life seemed to have wrapped up my childhood that very day. Afghanistan had not remained a safe place for people like my father to stay and practise their way of life. He was maybe among the last living men from Afghanistan who had the good fortune of having been educated at Cambridge and implemented their knowledge in their own country for the good of its own people. After all, he belonged to the erstwhile royal family of Afghanistan. Being responsible and concerned about the welfare of his people came naturally to him. That night he had planned a small celebration, inviting all who lived in the neighbourhood. Two guests shot at him as he embraced to welcome them. It would be easier for you to relate if I called them Taliban; but for us they were neighbours who lived four houses away from ours."

"I am sorry to hear that. It must have been very hard for you to witness such a scene at that tender age." I was honestly feeling bad for the wrong turn Rosha's life had taken on that fateful day.

In consolation I said to her, "I lost my mother, moments after I was born. However, it was years later that I understood the loss I had inherited at my birth itself. As for you, it must have taken you days before you might have even shed a teardrop. Were you around the place when it happened?" I asked just wanting to know how normal people feel when they face their dear ones, aware that they would depart with the next breath or two.

In thirty-seven years of my life, I had seen at least a score of criminals, terrorists breathe their last in front of my eyes. Whenever that had happened, I had felt that in a way the dying had released him from a trap he could not have otherwise gotten out of himself. I had never faced any of my family members die in front of my eyes. I had never wept on anybody's death or later. I always thought all of them had led a full life, and had lived to see more than they could have wished or imagined.

Besides as per my personal rulebook – One should get used to the reality of death as early as possible, because everyone will have to depart one day or the other. Therefore, instead of feeling remorse for the departed, one should congregate to share memories of the good times they had spent together. I know it is easier said than done, but how much more would the human brain need to evolve emotionally to understand this basic fact and find a justified solution to tackle such an unconquerable reality?

Learning that even I had grown up with the loss of a parent, Rosha somehow connected with me more on an individual, personal level, rather than to a law-keeper.

"I at least had a full family of an elder sister, and two younger brothers along with my parents and me. It must have been very difficult for you as a child."

She commented with genuine concern and a moment later, she flinched, "Please don't think that I am saying this to appease you. I..."

I waved my hand interrupting her justification and replied, "Don't worry about me; I am a father of two children myself now. Being a father myself, I can relate to the fears that your father might have had in his last moments, and the hardship you would have had to go through," I said wondering genuinely what I would feel if I were to find myself in that very position some day as of Rosha's father.

Our little pit stop had put us at ease with each other. We had to resume our journey once again. We shuffled our seating positions. Rosha and I sat facing each other on the back seat while one of my colleagues took the seat next to the other woman and the third next to the driver.

"At fourteen it's a very challenging period for the child. I mean one is stepping into adolescence, and that's when one needs the parental support to the fullest." Rosha looked at me and I noticed that her dead stare had faded away. Her pristine eyes had for some reason, regained life in them. I could see them react for the first time.

"So where were you when all that happened?" I questioned her reminding, where we had left the real discussion.

"I was in my bedroom. My mother and sister were dressing me up for the occasion. My father always told me that I was an angel. For some reason, he would feel very peaceful on having a glimpse of me," replied Rosha, with her mind travelling back into her bedroom and imaging the atmosphere, wherein she must have been pampered and well looked after.

One could notice the authenticity of her love and respect Rosha had for her father, for her face would begin to glow at a mention of him.

"He was a big man, a large-hearted Pathan in the true sense. He had earned great respect for his struggle to oust the Russians. Later, he had managed to raise funds and made three schools in and around Kabul. My father firmly believed that if the orphaned children of those who laid their lives for the nation were not provided with an opportunity to educate themselves, then a day would soon bring us to face a new revolt of some other kind. He was not a politician and still led a very hectic public life.

"Whenever he would return home angered by something or somebody he would call for me first. As I would enter his room, he would stretch his arms to hug me, place me on his lap, and speak to me about anything I wanted to. But at the end of it all, when it was time for him to leave, he would always kneel in front of me and kiss my hands and say those words – My Angel.

"That night I was wearing a special dress he had managed to get ready especially for the occasion. It was a beautiful white gown made from the best satin available and a pair of wings. Whenever I remember that day, I cannot ignore the irony."

Rosha turned silent for a moment and then continued, "We heard the gunshots and assumed that someone had fired a few in the air in celebration. It is a very common practice out there. What drew our attention was the shocking silence that followed the gunshots. That seemed peculiar and that is when my mother glanced out of the window and screamed. As we rushed out into the garden, I saw my father sitting rested against a wall, covering his wound with a hand that was smeared with his blood still flowing out of the wounds in his chest. He looked at me, smiled and stretched the other hand towards me, calling me closer. A few of his close aids helped him kneel one last time. I was so shocked seeing all that had happened that I plainly walked close to my father and held his hand, he looked at me, smiled and kissed my hands saying those words – My Angel, before lying down with a smile.

"He kept looking at me and me at him. It was as if time had frozen shortly, until the wailing women stormed to the other side to revive my mother who fainted with shock. An elderly guest shut my father's eyelids chanting some holy verse. Only then did I realise that he was no more. I should have left with him that day if I were truly an angel. Since I am not one, I was destined to live and die many deaths myself." Rosha turned calm and silent; her aquamarine blue-green eyes seemed like the gentle surface of an ocean that had furious undercurrents hidden deep within.

Gazing out of the window of our car, I could see the road speed away in the opposite. It was very similar to Rosha's life that had sped away her growing up years much faster than they should have, leaving her stranded on the crossroads from where it is hard for me to imagine how she must have decided which way to go. The past of nine years was going to take its own time to tell and we had already covered half the distance to our destination. I realised I had about an hour and a half to extract all I could out of Rosha.

Just then, I questioned myself; why was I so curious to know about her? Besides what was I going to do about it anyways? I decided that I would deal with my questions to myself on the way back. Now, I wanted to know more about Case Number ADT147/12/08, meaning Rosha.

5

A Fatal Compromise

"It is beyond my comprehension to face the fact that a man who rose to save a clan, further to be revered as a hero, was killed by those very men who had accorded him that honour one day," I remarked to Rosha. I continued, "At the same time I cannot forget a similarly shameful fact from our own history when someone had mustered the courage to shoot at the father of our nation."

"In fact, I feel my father's death proved his prophecies. Since the Russians left, he had been initiating education and rehabilitation camps and centres for the children so that they could be trained to think in a manner where they could merge with the ocean of humanity one day, blend with the mainstream rather than restrict themselves to be known as some member of a tribe alone. Since my father had not failed in his efforts till then, opportunistic and radical preachers of faith found it justified to have him eliminated," said Rosha.

Her eyes welled up as she spoke further, "Those very people, who must have approved his murder, became his pallbearers. Those very men gave speeches of my father's stature to have risen to that of a martyr. Those very people were not going to be satisfied with just that much. They wanted to make sure that none of us survived in time to come. The soldiers who had once fought the Russians and saved our nation were now wielding guns to save a religion that seemed threatened. Talibanisation was in its infant state and my father's murder was one of the early examples they set for the rest to understand that if a head did not bow to their diktat then it would not rest on its shoulders for long. My father rubbished the Talibs openly so one day they made him bite the dust." Rosha suddenly grew silent as if the scenes from the yore were right in front of her eyes, and once again, she was preparing herself to believe that life without a father was going to be very daunting.

"I am sorry as it must have been very hard on the whole family and for you at that age. How did you all manage after your father's death?" I asked.

"In less than a month after my father's death, we were left with almost nothing to manage, besides the house, my mother, my elder sister and our maid. My mother had wept so much, and for so long that her tear bags must have run dry. First she wept for the loss of her husband, and soon enough, she had to for the loss of her two sons. My younger brother who was almost thirteen then, disappeared one fine day. Some said that the Talibs had taken him away but the youngest one had managed to slip away. In any case, neither did we find him nor did he ever return. Officer, if you thought that trauma would have ended with that for us then you have to wait to learn how meaninglessly brutal and two-faced, morality and faith can be when it comes to bending rules for one's own conveniences," said Rosha.

Worse than what I could have imagined had already happened in her life so far. What could be beyond I wondered, maintained silence and let her go on.

Rosha narrated, "One day our mother woke us up earlier than usual and asked us to help her clean the house, and proper it as we were expecting guests. My sister and I assumed that it must be some distant relative who must be paying us a condolence visit or something of that nature. After a good two months from that tragic night, our home seemed to regain its order. It looked like it had looked before the tragedies. The only noticeable difference was that for some unknown reasons, flowers had stopped blooming in our courtyard. My father was very fond of them and it was also the other way round. It seemed that they were still in mourning. Having said that we had just about gathered ourselves to start all over once again, a spate of disasters had left us for death too.

"That day even though we worked very hard to proper the house, our mother seemed remorseful and withdrawn. Zeba, our maid had borrowed some snacks from someone's house I guessed, to offer to the guests who were expected. What gave rise to our curiosities further was that we were ordered to wear bright and colourful clothes. It was beyond my comprehension but for some reason my elder sister, who was seventeen by then agreed, so did I. Aashna, my elder sister, seemed to have an inkling of what was to follow; I always looked up to her as she was the wisest amongst all of us and the prettiest too. That day she readied me with her own hands as my mother preferred to retire, and grab a nap before the guests arrived. No matter how many times I questioned my sister, she did not let her fears be known to me.

"That afternoon, two Arabs accompanied by a local from Kabul arrived at our house. All of them were around the age of my father. Zeba handed us over trays filled with snacks and *sherbet,* both of us sisters walked across our living room serving them all that we had and borrowed from elsewhere. They looked at us in a way no one had before. I did not know what was going on, but my sister did. Her intuitions had never failed her and with every passing minute, she kept confirming her doubts.

"As we peered through the *pardah,* we could see our mother wiping away her tears from time to time, with Zeba by her side, comforting my mother and wiping her own tears too. While the humanitarian messenger from Kabul counselled the hapless ladies that in given situation that we had found ourselves in, how long would we manage to survive, and save ourselves from the sex starving men on the street? He continued to convince my mother that at least this way we would be assured of a comfortable life. The preferable age of girl for such a trade off in middle-eastern countries was eleven or twelve years. We both had surpassed the norm, but we did not remain unsold. Our mother was faced with a gruesome choice to make – See us being raped, multiple times and by multitudes of men until we die, or permit us to be raped by one man for life if that man was ready to take the responsibility to take care of us. Did she have the courage to bear our rape and death too? I don't say that the pimp was totally wrong in his reasoning, but then was this the only way left at humanity's disposal to rid us of our tyranny? It took me long time before I could forgive that pimp." Rosha ended her monologue and became silent as if the silence communicated her surrender better than words could have.

I wonder why fate makes such ruthless moves on people who deserve it the least. Rosha's silence compelled me to hear all those screams, her cries and wailing in solitude but somewhere I hoped that it was just my imagination. Someone would have stood between the family, and I was filled with anger and disgust for those ruthlessly moneyed masters who believe that everything on the earth is gettable as long as one can negotiate a price for it.

"So did you two leave with those men?" Eight words of my question seemed like climbing eight steps down into hell.

Rosha looked at me, into my eyes, trying to judge my character, wanting to know what could I be more interested in hearing – the wanton fantasies of the wealthy Arabs or the agony hidden wrapped around their women from head to toe?

"Yes," she replied bowing her eyes in shame.

It took me a while to gather my voice. "Rosha, you do not need to feel ashamed of anything. You braved through it so far. I am sure you will see the light of day," I said gripping her hand in mine, tightly, reassuring her that I honestly felt that ways for her.

"Officer, you have no idea what I had escaped from, so don't even try to predict a fate that can never be my future once I board that aircraft you are going to put me on to."

She was stern. Her eyes conveyed her anger and helplessness together. "You haven't the slightest of idea what it feels to lie on a bed of roses with a man as old as your own father, tearing your clothes just like a lion tears open his kill. His hunger, his desperation gives way to grace and aesthetics. That was my first death. I thought I was done with it once and for all after the ordeal was over, but once again, I was wrong."

Rosha seemed unstoppable. She might have realised that this could well be her last chance of sharing her agonies wholeheartedly, and I realised that we as a modern society had been exceptionally hasty in assuming that such trade-offs had become a thing o the past.

"Within a week from when those Arabs came to see us first, my sister and I were ready to leave Kabul for good. She was to live in Kuwait while I in Riyadh. All said and done, the new millennium transformed us from bubbly and loving innocent daughters to concubines of the wealthy masters who had seemingly well compensated our mother.

"We parted the same way that we would have if we were to get married and leave that house with our husbands. For our mother and Zeba, it felt the same way, only we two sisters knew where we were going was not a home but a harem. Yet, love had filled our lives so much until then that tears seemed apparent and unstoppable.

"The house frontage seemed like as though our father had broadened his torso and was standing there bidding us goodbye silently. My sister kept saying to me that she would not live there for long and would return soon. I wondered how she was going to manage that. As we stepped into the car that drove us to the airport, I took it for granted that this was the last time I was ever going to see my mother, Zeba, my house and my homeland.

"As we arrived at the airport, neither my sister nor I were prepared to bid each other goodbye instantly. Unfortunately we had to as the chartered jet sent by her master waited, all fuelled and ready to lift off with my sister as the new flavour for his carnal pleasures. We looked into each other's eyes, hugged and surprisingly not a teardrop spilled out from either of our eyes. We had understood that we were on our own from here on, and thus weakness would not help. We had to be strong if we needed to face the true world along with its gruesome realities. We both parted in a gap of an hour or so. That was the last day of childhood and the same day a few hours later I was to turn an adult."

❑❑❑

6

In the Prison of Gold

Manipulated confessions always have the same beginning, middle and end, no matter how many times you question the guilty. That is when we know that the suspect is lying, for emotions do not generally spill themselves in a chronicled fashion. Rosha was indeed speaking the truth. She was revealing her memories in the order they were coming to her. Thus, the most gruesome incidents occurred to her mind before other memories that reminded her of that gory night, and before she could even reveal anything about the man that had bought her. Moments later, she did get to that and I remained an ardent listener.

"I had hardly managed to get any sleep that night. One, because I had no idea of what sexual exploitation meant until then, and two, because of the physical and mental pain it had caused. I felt that I had been looted of all that I stood for, and that was meant to be offered by me to someone I would think was deserving of it. Unfortunately though, thugs had plundered me and left with the loot.

"When I woke up next morning, I was startled to see myself surrounded by women from all sides. Before I could scream in panic they comforted me and explained that they were my family from that day on. There were twenty women beside me in that room. None of them seemed to have stepped over the third decade of their lives. All of them belonged to my master's harem. As they gave me a bath and applied perfumed oils on my body, some had tears in their eyes. Probably they had gone through similar rituals when they must have arrived, I thought.

"Many would have been purchased under the same circumstances as me. As time passed I learnt that my master had a harem of about twenty women then. Many had withered away like old furniture in the past, only the ones that were there were of use to him. Each one was given a villa to live. My master was very particular in such matters. He knew that if all of us would stay under the same roof, one of us would surely conspire his doom sooner or later. In a week's time or so I was shunted to a plush villa that I was to call home from that day on.

"I guess with time, my master had mastered his skills of extracting everything from within a person and then doctor their wounds with luxuries that could make hundreds envy you rather than pity your plight. The thought of drawing blood would give him an unimaginable high. It would transform him from a mere mortal to an undying beast. He had drawn blood out of each one of us and did something very similar for a living. He owned oil wells – drawing the earth's blood." The details of the lavish lure seemed inane, as the gruesome truth that hid behind it was not the one that deserved to be peeled, layer after layer. Thus, I did not interrupt and Rosha did not ponder.

"He had fathered almost a hundred children. I wonder if he were to run into his own son in the street, he would have difficulty recognising him as his own. One of his own daughters from his earlier wives was much older than I was then. It was unholy, unnatural, and inhumane and all that counts for exploitation of the weakest, but then, in the end that is what always happens. The weak lose their voice, their will, their might and slave for the rest of their lives…" Rosha had once again slipped into silence as though with time she had tempered her mind to surrender to the will of her master. As though she had accepted the repetitive gruesome act to be her present and future, until she had lost the purpose she had been brought there for.

"I hope you didn't surrender altogether, did you?" I asked soon enough, not wasting much time in speculating my afterthoughts as time was running out on us. Soon I would be officiating Rosha's departure, and try to protect her from the prying eyes of the cops and constables at the airport.

"Believe it or not I had in fact surrendered. I was shattered.

I did not think of killing myself only because my father had deeply ingrained it in our minds that suicide was the tool of the cowardly. While for the mighty, they brave their way through circumstances with the help of wisdom and efforts. My faith in my father's words had also begun to dwindle, but then it all started to fall back in place gradually."

We were approaching a rest area and I was in desperate need of a cigarette. I ordered the driver accordingly, and forced in a little more time to satisfy my curiosity a little further. All my colleagues turned around to look at me, wondering why I needed a stop again. Rosha was sharp in such matters. No wonder she asked me bluntly, "Why do you wish to make another stop? Aren't you satisfied with all that I have told you so far? Would you let me continue to live here if I told you everything?"

Her questions struck me like bullets. As I reminisce those moments, I feel in a way I too was exploiting her by extracting her past out of her. Similar to her Arab master, I too was drawing blood out of that anaemic carcass to satisfy my own thirst.

"I am sorry if you felt that ways, but to be honest I badly need a smoke therefore the stop; besides I am not forcing you to speak. It's your wish."

The car halted in the parking lot. We stepped out and I lit a cigarette. With its first drag, I knew that I had not been completely honest in my last answer and I had no qualms in admitting it to myself.

When we began our journey, I had never expected that the following two or three hours would reveal a lifetime one had spent, compelling you to find out more. I was a custodian of law but I was human too, who had sentiments, emotions and concern for others in him. I would never think twice before I arrested a criminal. However, in Rosha's case, here the guilty, meaning her Arab master was not being punished. Instead, the innocent, meaning Rosha had already served time. What kind of justice could this mean? I wondered as I puffed away the cancer stick and got into our little time-tube once again surrendering to Rosha's will to take me wherever she wished to go next in time that had very little beauty in it, no serenity, only the simmering barren sands of Saudi Arabia wherein Rosha seemed like a fast evaporating oasis.

"I am sorry. I was rude to you," said Rosha as our car hit the road once again, speeding towards our destination.

"You don't need to be sorry, Rosha. After all you are making your final attempts to make a miracle possible but unfortunately you are telling about it, to a person who is bound to not let it happen, even though in his heart he prays that he should fail in his attempts this time at least," I said looking into her eyes.

Rosha's eyes turned moist once again and I turned to look away. I had no courage to face them.

"Don't worry officer, I have nothing against you. You are doing what is expected of you and as long as deep down in your heart you are convinced that I deserved a chance – I am happy. Not everybody in this world gets a chance to triumph even if they deserve one. I would be one of those unfortunate ones."

Oh! Her words… her words made me realise how powerless I could be too in certain situations. I wonder at times that probably life had made me go through such an event only to remind me of my limitations. It was probably for me to learn that the king and the pawn end up in the same wooden box after the game was over. None of the two is anything more than sculpted blocks of wood until they regain their repute once they are placed on the chessboard.

The chequered life of Rosha was to teach me all that I could anticipate further and beyond. Even though Rosha had accepted to spend her time in that gilded prison, she had not given up the desire to escape. Only if she knew the tools she needed to set her free and only if she got them in time. It was time alone that could once again reveal what it had in store to offer.

❑❑❑

7

A Key to Freedom

"You know officer, back in our land, we believe that when one feels like revealing all about one's own life to a complete stranger; it means that the person is nearing the end of his life." I was about to react to that statement from Rosha, but she had gone back into her yesteryears once again and signalled me not to interrupt.

"I turned sixteen in that villa. Two years had gone by turning me into a mere trophy that rested on a mantelpiece. When it catches someone's attention, it's brought down, handled, looked from all sides, praised for its beauty and then once again it is returned to its resting place. Besides tending to my master's needs, I loved looking after a little garden that I had managed to create in the blazing desert heat. I would also read for long hours at a stretch.

"I had brought some books that once belonged to my father and my master had noticed me reading on several occasions. He had not stopped me from pursuing my hobbies. Little did he know that those books would help me wander in a different world altogether. A world that did not exist for me at that time but it surely existed somewhere for real. That was the sum and all of my life for almost two years, until that night when my master stormed into my villa, intoxicated and furious.

"He was an animal indeed, but I had never seen that look on his face before. That night he did not handle me like a trophy. That night he looked at me as if I were a traitor who had betrayed his trust and goodness. That is what he screamed at me. I looked at him, released myself from his grip, and took a seat, not paying heed to his annoyance. Inside, deep within myself I was scared and wondered what I had done to call for such wrath. I did not beg or plead at his feet for mercy, and he went on blabbering with a heavy slur in his voice, giving me some idea of how much liquor he must have had to muster up courage to speak to me in the way he was at that moment. At the end of it all, he hurled glassware all around, and shattered everything that caught his eye and left.

"I had not understood a thing from that act until a few days later when I was driven to a hospital for a thorough check-up. Even though I wondered where I was going, I forgot it soon as it was the first time in two years that I had travelled out of my home in broad daylight. It was also the first time when I saw the city in sunshine. It was beautiful but every now and then, whenever a veiled woman would cross my sight, I would wonder, could that be another Rosha hiding behind that garb or could she be a fortunate soul who leads a life of dignity?

"Because the world I had become a part of, was a world in which people did not believe in hiding shame. It was a world where women were nothing more than another means for deriving pleasure. In the bargain, how the woman was feeling about the whole thing, could not have been the last question, even that could have crossed the minds of the pleasure seeker.

"When I met with one other woman from the Arab's harem at the hospital, I was surprised. After a usual exchange of pleasantries, she told me that she was there to assist me with the medical tests that I was to undergo. First, I was curious to know why I was brought to a hospital, and secondly, I wondered what tests I were to go through and for what. After a lot of persuasion, she turned to look in my eyes. Over the years, she must have realised that sympathy was not a good virtue as it did not help heal our wounds, rather would infect deeper and turn us insane. She revealed that one of our master's women had taunted him about his failing vigour. She supported her claim with the fact that I had not managed to fertilise yet. The way my master's escort looked at me after revealing that fateful secret, I knew that my fate was sealed as theirs had been, years ago.

"At the hospital, I understood the reason of my master's madness, a few nights ago. The doctor was very kind to me and conducted a battery of tests. Later when she wrote down my age on some form, she looked at me once just as any mother would, and questioned me authoritatively, 'You are still a child and you want a child so soon?' A sudden chill ran down my spine. It had never even crossed my mind that this could have happened long ago. Next moment, I wondered why it had not. I had questions to one problem while found answers for another. My reaction and answer were as warranted as they should have been. I told the doctor that I was nobody to decide against my master's will, well aware that I was accompanied by one other loyal of his.

"Thankfully the doctor did not enquire about my relation with the other, but tried reasoning with her too about my tender age, and physical inability to bear a child as yet. My companion maintained a look that hinted the doctor that she could not understand one single word that was said to her so far. The doctor was Dutch, probably in her late forties and she shook her head in a way suggesting how hard it was for her to comprehend my plight. She said, 'If your husband is in such a rush, then tell him to bring another wife, as you might never be able to breed, my girl.' She mistook my expressions to be that of shock and dismay, whereas in fact I was so relieved to know that I was barren. I was overjoyed by the fact that I would never bear him a child, which he would have difficulty in remembering or recognising. After all I must have finished paying my dues to whatever I might have donc to deserve such a life, I thought.

"That evening, back at my place as I showered, I felt the water was cleansing me of all the grime and stench of salivating inhumanity that had stuck to me like a coat. The fingerprints of those hands that had textured my skin all over, that stinking smell of his sweat, which I had got used to breathe day after day – it seemed all to have washed away that evening."

Even though Rosha spoke of relief, it was hard for me to foresee, how all this would free her from the shackles she had gotten into. I interrupted her with my question, "I do not understand what made you think that you were freed from the duties of that heinous life you were made to live."

Rosha's eyes glistened playfully like a child who was about to whisper 'A secret' into the ears of her best friend triumphantly.

"I told everything about me to that doctor at the hospital. She was so shocked and angered that she did not bat an eyelid to alter my reports. She hid away the facts under a cryptic maze of words in such a way that to the reader it may seem as though I was still too young and my ovaries were still developing to be capable to fertilise. On the other hand, it deserved a healthy sperm count from the mate too. Therefore, while the report offered me the handicap of time, it ruthlessly declared my master to be heading towards impotency."

Looking at her face light up for the first time, I could imagine how happy she must have been on that day. Out of nowhere, she had managed to find a saviour. For those few moments, even I was thrilled, dismissing reality and enjoy imaging that Arab dealing with the prickly judgement that had come his way.

From that day on Rosha did not have to cater to her master's whims. He was done with her and contemplated what he had done to deserve this. Paying obeisance in the court of the Almighty, begging for mercy, was a solution he thought. Rosha felt liberated two years after she had become a victim of gruesome destiny.

When one finds oneself surrounded by unthinkable peril, it is of no use to think of solutions that work as an antidote under normal circumstances. For the situation Rosha was in, time, fate and all other elements physically, metaphysically existing in Nature had to come together to hand her a hint, which if she used correctly, could result in her freedom and if she let it pass then she would continue to live there with the knowledge of her being barren and the fear – what if her master was to throw her out of his harem.

On the other hand, I thought that she was offered the clue only because she was capable to grasp it and make use of it. No wonder others did not have such an option in their time. That is why lives of every individual seems unique and fate seems generous to a few and miserly to plenty. Little do the complaining individuals realise that they lacked the sight to see, and the mind to grasp when fate might have been generous to them too. This vital fact is the root cause of cultivating unthinkable numbers of people who come up with unthinkable solutions to various problems humankind has faced.

As I shared my thoughts with Rosha, she realised that I was genuinely elated for her and before I could go on with my thoughts further, she interrupted me with a question. "Officer, how far or close are we from the airport?"

Her question shook me out of the world she had transported me to. I looked out of the window and replied, "About an hour or so."

I realised Rosha wanted to speak further and I needed to give her the opportunity and keep my opinions to myself for the moment.

❑❑❑

8

Hope, Fear & Friendship

Rosha must have taken days to convince herself that her master might not visit her anytime soon after receiving the doctor's judgement. "I would at times wake up from sleep whenever I would hear a car pass by, thinking that he must have arrived. To my relief, my nightmares remained just nightmares for the time being," said Rosha.

At last, the simmering sands had not managed to encroach all over the oasis turning it into hot steam. Nature does have its balance of winds, heat, dust, and rain. This balance of Nature had mysteriously guarded the existence of an oasis named Rosha.

When hope blossoms to full bloom, it expects to bear fruit called achievement. While Rosha, meaning hope indulges herself in preparation to bear the fruit, she forgets the world around her, therefore it is not hard for her to ignore revenge that had been lurking around, waiting for an opportunity to get the better of her.

What followed from Rosha was something of that kind and more. In her case, revenge had teamed up with anger and abuse. Revenge, alias the Arab, had an undefeatable and lethal combination on its side, while hope, meaning Rosha, was happily unaware of its presence.

"After two years I had found time to remorse the death of my father and separation from my family. As the tide of my tears ended, I realised how long and far I had come from home. Expecting to go back was obvious, but to go back to what, was the question, to which I could not seem to find an answer.

"I had spent two years and over in a state of loose-consciousness I guess. No wonder all these thoughts had never occurred to me before. Somewhere within me, I was aware of the existence of the real Rosha gasping for breath, and I was not ready to let her die. With my limited resources I had nursed her so far, but how was I going to continue?"

Rosha suddenly went into that space that might have traumatised her before and turned silent for the moment as if giving her listener – me – time to prepare for what was to follow.

When one has to choose between hope and fear, one generally surrenders to fear and accepts what comes his way. Unfortunately that would form the destiny of Rosha I guessed, as she did not have anything to fall back on and very little she could do without quoting her master's name. My training, analytical skills and experience did not prevent me from transforming myself into a normal human being and hoped that fate would have realised its folly and corrected itself now at least.

I asked her, "So did you return to Afghanistan?"

She glanced at me and commented callously, "You must have connected by browsing through the pages of my passport."

It is strange but true that whenever a hardened criminal decides to improve, we tend to suspect him of driving us into a trap. In this case, Rosha thought I was luring her. Even though I later realised that she was not at fault, but today when one thinks of it as a whole, one has to accept the fact that somewhere on that journey, we had surrendered to each other without any inhibitions, flaws and shortfalls put together. If we had agreed to listen to each other, empathise with one another, guide one another, then we were also ready to fight one another, insult and abuse one another; and that is what I did after her comment.

"So far all I have gathered about you from the documents is, your name and nationality you possess. If I knew anything further about you, do you think it would be giving me any pleasure listening to your luck-lost tale so far? You must be thinking that by making you converse I am confirming the statistics in your passport. If I needed to do that, you would not be sitting in front of me and heading to the airport, do you understand!" With that, I had returned to being who I was and Rosha had returned to being a deportee.

The pitch of my voice, Rosha's silence and the blending tones of my snoring colleagues made me wonder, was it necessary for me to terrorise the poor thing? Today, when I judge it, I think it was.

A friendship needs to stand on the foundation of love, encouragement, care, belonging and so on. Along the way, should one friend get angered at the other when one has mistaken or misunderstood the other, then one should have the liberty to react, while for the other to realise that he cares, therefore such reaction.

What Rosha had said had angered me. After all, I was not infuriated by a comment from a nobody. I had taken her to be a friend by then... a friend who I could probably help in the future and maybe some day, when she had settled in life, visit her in her house, where she would host me as a friend, brother, and my children would play with hers as their own cousins.

Unfortunately, though, she had misunderstood and I was not ready to ask further after my outburst. Thus, silence reigned supreme, as we both waited for an external force to intervene.

As time passed, we kept heading closer and closer to the airport with every passing minute. I had cooled down in the meanwhile, and was about to give in, well aware of the fact that I personally do not like unsolved mysteries. As I was coming to terms with my ego, and rest of the emotions that might have been hurt then, Rosha was also making peace with herself.

"I am sorry to have hurt you," she said.

"In fact I should have controlled my temper," I replied.

Indeed, we had become friends by saying a line each to the other. For that's all that it takes to let the other person know – All said and done, I love you and had no intention to hurt you. So let's go back to being friends again!

I looked at my watch and told Rosha that we were soon approaching the end of our journey. "We have another forty-five minutes to go, give or take, ten minutes more. Would you be able to bring yourself from Saudi Arabia to here and now in that much time?"

Rosha smiled, she was at complete ease with me by then. "Officer, I am just twenty-two years old, of which I have already shared sixteen. How long would it take me to tell you about the remaining six?"

I waved my palms had at her signalling, "Well, then go on."

❑❑❑

9

Treacherous Retribution

"After a layover of two months I had a car waiting in the porch one evening. I knew what it meant and I understood that it was time to return to hell once again. Probably my master must have got a second opinion from another doctor and must have felt relieved or maybe he must have credited the Almighty of having pulled off a miracle for him. As I dressed for the evening, countless thoughts crossed my mind but not one was close to what I was going to face that night.

"I was driven across the city into the desert sands where my master had camped with a few friends of his. He had earned the reputation of being one of the best hosts in Saudi Arabia for the extravagance and splendour he showered over his guests.

Huge tents had been erected. Carpets, chandeliers, fruits, food, alcohol seemed to be in abundance. As I was escorted to a tent, I saw beautiful Egyptian belly dancers preparing themselves to welcome the night with their exotic dance.

"One thing that seemed strange though, I was not able to spot any other woman who belonged to the harem. There were plenty of women of all possible races, but none that I had known or met before. Something within me warned me that it was not going to be a usual fare. My instincts sensed that life was going to turn another leaf that night.

"It was well past midnight and I was sitting out of my tent, gazing at the starlit sky. A gentle breeze had cooled off my fears for the moment and the music emanating from the main tent worked like a lullaby for me. I was once again at ease with myself and nothing seemed to bother me. I don't remember when I dozed off that night and for how long, but that night, after so many years I dreamed of being in my house in Kabul. Everything seemed to be the way it used to be. As if, nothing had happened and all was routine.

"Even though I watched myself in the dream, I was conscious of the fact that it was a dream and was very happy to see my whole family come alive in front of my eyes. I remember seeing myself tending to my father's favourite rose bushes. While I learnt how important it was to till the soil without damaging the roots of the plants, my father would inspect my work and move his hand over my head like a blessing. While that is what I was enjoying in my dream, somebody was actually tapping my shoulder.

"I sensed that it was for real; somebody was indeed trying to wake me. I could hear a faint voice as if telling me 'let's go, enough of dreams for now… come on let's go'. It was hard to break a dream wherein I was reuniting with my family after such a long gap. Thus, it did take me a while to return to reality. I woke up to see one of my master's men standing close to me and signalling that I had been summoned to the main tent. As I prepared to walk back to my tent, I wondered what was to follow. What eventually followed was worse than a nightmare. Standing there in that tent that night I realised that waking out of a soothing, gentle dream is the sign of a hard shock to follow in reality.

"The night I lost my father, I thought I would always remember it as the most horrendous night of my life. Then came a night when I surrendered myself to my master for the first time and added it to my list of horrendous memories. That night when I readied myself and looked at myself in the mirror, I thought to myself that I was surely going to add up another night to the list.

"There I was standing amongst the other women while about fifteen men or my master's esteemed guests, roved their eyes from top to bottom over our bodies, imaging those covered portions of our bodies and imagining who could be well her worth to spend the night with. As I stood there, shocked, just as I was when my mother had to let us go, I glanced once or twice at my master; the look in his eyes was enough for me to realise that this was his way of avenging the insult I had brought upon him. Without speaking a word to me, he had communicated that if he could afford to shower me with luxuries, then he could also beat me to dust, he wanted me to be reminded of my true position – that I was his slave.

"That night I had transformed from being a mistress of a wealthy Arab to a comfort woman of his guests. My master never shared his women with anybody, even though he would flaunt them, but that too just to make others appreciate his taste of things as he would put it often."

Rosha stopped speaking suddenly as though that night had come alive in her mind all over again and in front of her eyes. Her eyes welled up. She wanted to continue but she had lost the courage.

"You don't need to speak about it if you don't wish to; it's alright," I said to her.

"No officer, just give me a moment please. I need to get out with it once and for all. You know, it is one thing to stand naked in front of a man but being stripped by several, and that too while they know that you are not too comfortable with it; I consider it to be a mass rape of sanity. That is the price I had to pay for deceiving my master." Rosha delicately wiped the welling tears and took a moment to herself.

I seemed at loss of words. How was I to comfort a girl who had seen so much, had been abused beyond reason and was now rendered hapless in front of salivating men, who must have surely earned great repute themselves to be on that Arab's guest list?

I wondered how inhumane such reputed men truly were to be able to indulge in such sadistic and atrocious exploitation.

Do people forget that they too were born to a woman? They too must have fallen in love with a woman and they too must have fathered daughters that could one day, God forbid, trade themselves to circumstance. Does the sight of naked women numb the mind of such men to such an extent that compassion or concern just fails to occur to them at all? What could I say, when I had questions and had plenty of them storming my mind? As a man, I was feeling ashamed of what Rosha might have gone through that night.

Then suddenly it occurred to me that why had fate offered her respite if it had decided to lead her to total gloom? My question compelled me to think what else could have happened that night besides the obvious. The only miraculous reference that came to my mind, I shared it with Rosha.

"You know that reminds me of a very similar situation that once occurred in *Mahabharata,* it's a mythological..." I said as she interrupted me.

"I know, I have read it. Fortunately, Draupadi had Krishna rescue her from the brink of humiliation she would have otherwise had to go through. As for me, I was surrounded by scores of Duryodhanas, who tore me apart like the hyenas battle for leftover meat. You know, officer, why I insisted on telling you all that I just said? Because in that pack of hyenas, one was to become my saviour, my Krishna."

"I am surprised to know that you are aware of Indian mythology," I said to her complimenting her knowledge and trying not to ponder too much on the episode, she had just finished narrating.

"Actually I studied it in my Theology classes. I also know fairly about the *Vedas, Upanishads,* and *Ramayana*. It was all a part of our Oriental Religions study class."

I was dumbstruck. Here was a girl, who had barely known herself when she had to depart from her loved ones for good with a memory full of death, wounds, and a sordid separation. Then she went through an ordeal that even she could not have imagined. After going through all that malevolence, I wondered how she could end up taking classes in Theology.

Life indeed is not a drive on a straight road. It has its fair share of uphill drives, slopes, and hairpin bends. Each one of us has had an experience of it and will continue to gather more as we travel further. For some reasons though, I felt that Rosha had travelled too far in too little time. Did it mean that she was nearing her end? On the other hand, could she eventually become a writer, as she hoped? I did not have a definite answer for either of my questions back then.

Today I do and its revelation can wait for some time, as the oasis named Rosha was about to evaporate and escape the torturous hot sands of Saudi Arabia, like a cloud blown to new lands with the hope of starting afresh.

❑❑❑

10

The Offer

Cocooned as a sex slave in Saudi Arabia, Rosha had transformed into a colourful butterfly that fluttered in and out of classrooms and libraries of an ancient college in the United Kingdom.

Rosha's transition was equally wondrous as the myriad colours sprinkled on the wings of a butterfly. She thrived on the nectar of knowledge. With the passing of time, scars of her dreadful past had begun to heal and disappear. Fear could no longer intimidate her thoughts. Even though all of it seemed very enchanting, I thought that she had skipped a few memories in between. Maybe they were too brutal to recollect or probably too shameful to share.

"Don't you think you have forgotten the bridge in the middle?" I hinted her.

She was sharp. Her eyes expressed her naughtiness as she said smilingly, "I was just making sure, if you were really interested in listening any further as most of the X-rated scenes of my story are over."

We both had a hearty laugh at that. For a moment, we had forgotten all that had brought us together and all that would separate us soon. At that moment, we both were just like friends laughing over casual banter.

"That night in tent the person who saved me was Edward, a young British businessman. His father and my master had business relations going back years. Edward was learning the ropes of the business he would soon inherit from his father. In the company, among men of the age of my father and grandfather, fondling girls and women suited to be their granddaughters, Edward seemed to be truly young and embarrassed. In all the sleaze and chaos, I had managed to glance at him a few times and wondered what was wrong with him, when others were devouring us like hungry beasts.

"I guessed he must have been in his late twenties. He for some reasons had sensed my uneasiness. While he kept sipping Champagne, he borrowed a few glances at me. He sensed my reluctance to the whole act and realised that I was not one of the usual whores who would throw themselves on anybody for money. He knew that I was suffocating in that atmosphere and he too was feeling claustrophobic I thought.

"My master kept glancing at me from time to time. His face lit up when Edward walked up to him and whispered something into his ear. My master had finally found the ultimate weapon to humiliate me, he thought, as the two of them walked to me. 'Go get dressed and escort our guest to his hotel and take good care of him; he is just like a son to me,' my master instructed. I did as I was told.

"At the hotel, Edward told me that he was not comfortable with the scene and for reasons he knew that I was not either, thus he had asked me out as a handy pretext for him to make a quick exit. I asked Edward if I was just going to remain a pretext or was I expected to.... Edward was a shy person. He did not force himself on me, not that night and never after.

"From that night until Edward returned to London ten days later, I lived with him in his suite, and my master was content with the revenge he had plotted. What he did not know was that I had revealed all the gory details of the past two years to Edward in the meanwhile. It was not as though I was dying to tell my tale, but he had a way of getting around with things. He was a gentleman who knew how to conduct himself. I fell for his qualities, and he would often remark in amazement about the way I conducted myself after having gone through all that I had. Somehow, all that reminded me of my father on various occasions. My father too was a stickler for mannerisms and etiquettes.

"Back then, I was about to turn seventeen, while Edward was nearing his twenty-sixth birthday. There could not have been much in common for us to attract each other, but then I was not like a seventeen-year-old anymore. Two years in that harem and in the company of other women like me, my mind had started functioning like a thirty-year-old.

"This, I guess, Edward had sensed somewhere along and thus he spent his evenings in my company. We dined together, we lived in the same room, slept in the same bed, without Edward compelling me to oblige him, until one night, probably the seventh, when neither of us could hold back our emotions. That was the first time I should say, that I made love to a man. I had wilfully surrendered to passion.

"Even though I was a concubine since the past few years, I had never realised the pleasure or completeness one experiences when you blend yourself with the one you love to become one. Edward's touch was different. He was not desperate for anything. He let me grow out of my inhibitions and express myself the way I wanted to.

"Two days later when I accompanied him to the airport, he held my hand in his all the way. He was silent. Some thought kept him from speaking a word. After checking in at the airport he walked up to me to say goodbye, I thought, instead he asked me if I was willing to come with him to England.

"I was spellbound by Edward's proposition. All I was able to do was stand in front of him, stare into his eyes, and notice the sincerity with which he had made me the offer. Tears rolled down my cheeks. For a few moments, my imagination ran wild. My father's voice echoed in my thoughts. His descriptions of Cambridge, the countryside and the city of London played in my ears. I was shaken out of my thoughts when Edward wiped my tears and said, 'You could study there and a make a life for yourself.' 'But you think he will let me go,' I questioned Edward. 'The little that I know about your master is enough for me to assure you that he is not a person who will sacrifice millions of pounds worth of business for a keep, I am sorry I did not mean to insult you,' he said. 'You don't have to be sorry, I am aware of my position, why should one try to imagine otherwise?' 'Let me get things laid out for you in the meanwhile. When I return, that is a fortnight from now, I promise to free you from this evil bondage.' Edward assured me as he moved his palm over mine. I could understand all that Edward spoke through his eyes, asking me to trust him, as he would soon be back for me.

"Thus, Edward returned to England to prepare to salvage a life of an unfortunate girl he had begun to fancy, while I returned to my dreaded castle, waiting for my prince charming to rescue me."

Once again, high points and low points in memories had preceded the order and Rosha had spoken about her newfound hope and life even before revealing the means to it. That dreaded night had commenced with a dream that Rosha had and the whole affair from thereon, until Edward left her with a dream to nurse.

She had dreamed of a family she had and would now imagine of a life she could lead. Fate, I admitted to myself, had a peculiar way of balancing itself. It is hard to fathom if one is not careful to connect events, incidents, one has gone past, to understand the logic behind this whole game called Life.

❑❑❑

11

He loves me, he loves me not

The days and nights Rosha spent waiting for Edward had made her very edgy.

As she put it, "One day I would wake up to the thought that he would keep his word and salvage me from this hell for ever. For hours, I would imagine a life for myself, which I had long forgotten to even dream of. I would wonder, plan things which I would like to do first and what later as if I was already in London.

"I would imagine the cityscape of London and find myself taking a walk in the Hyde Park, visiting Madame Tussauds museum, strolling down the Leicester Square, travelling across in the London Tube or the famous London cab. I would imagine taking pictures of myself with the Buckingham Palace in the backdrop. I could imagine all that due to the unfailing memories of my father, when he would gather me on his lap and then describe each place in such detail and show photographs of him in those places. Even though my sister and I would be awestruck by his experiences, he had always believed that one day we too would have the opportunity to experience the same. He believed that undertaking long journeys alone is very necessary for every individual to discover oneself completely. 'It turns a boy into a man,' he would say and my sister would answer back almost immediately, '*Abbajaan* we have no interest in turning ourselves into men.' That answer would suddenly bring him back to the real world and he would quickly correct himself, 'Oh! So it would help you turn from girls to charming young ladies. Don't you wish to be that at least?' All of us would have a hearty laugh at that.

"One day I would be reminded of my lost family and the good times we shared, another morning I would wake up from a nightmare in which I would see my father dying, I would witness my mother in a battered state, all alone hunting for her lost sons, my elder sister slaving her way through. I dreaded to wake up with such thoughts. Even though I knew it was just a dream, but then what I was looking forward to happen was no less than one either. Nightmares would, therefore, test my faith in Edward's word, and I would wonder all day long, what if he had just said it but not meant it? What if he did not come? What would I do? What could I do? The day would end up leaving me helpless and tired of thinking a way out of that hellhole. I don't know when, once again sleep would take me along with her on a mystical journey of dreams, nightmares and forecast my state of mind for the day to come.

"The wait was long and very hard. The life I had got used to in the past, was becoming unbearable by the passing days. I had started imaging myself as a student busy flipping through books, attending lectures, and all that my father had envisioned for me. Alas, if it were to be that ways, Edward would have arrived when he had said he would.

"The long wait between hope and despair started wearing off by the seventeenth or eighteenth day. I had begun to console myself that all said and done, at least I got a chance to live freely for ten days. Perhaps, I should not have got so attached to Edward and expressed myself so freely; but then I wondered – so what if I had? Otherwise, too, as per my master's command, I was bound to serve Edward in any way he pleased. I was convinced that I would cherish those moments, for those were the only good memories I had managed to gather since I had left home. The only thing that hurt about it was at the end of it all it seemed like a dream that could never come true.

"Two weeks turned into a month, Edward's face had begun to fade from my mind. I was beginning to lose my grip on the last hope that I was holding on to when one evening my master's car drove into my villa once again. My speculations, hopes and dreams ended there itself. As I walked across my bedroom to the washroom to prepare myself for that night, I consoled myself with the fact that no man had the courage or the will to return dignity to the woman that the men themselves had snatched away from her once. I was a glorified whore and was going to remain one for life, it's just that some men like to comfort you with soothing statements and have their way gracefully.

"If I were to meet anyone like Edward in future, I had decided to never take their words to heart. Just because one prefers foreplay of words doesn't make him better than the others who choose to... to consume us the moment we latched the door. My tears had washed away my reincarnated desire to begin once again. I readied myself and walked out of my room and onto the staircase to surrender myself to the gross reality.

"When I stepped into the living room, I froze at the sight my eyes saw. It took me a while to believe that Edward was really standing in front of me instead of my master. My heart pounded so loud that I could hear its reverb in my ears clearly. Joy did not seem to find a suitable expression to express. I could not just run towards my prince charming, hug him, weep in his arms, whine about the long and arduous wait or compel him to apologise even if he was not guilty of anything. In that house, I was my master's property and it had its ears and eyes that would report to its owner. I gathered myself, the storm of happiness that was building within me and behaved nothing more than courteous.

"Edward apologised for not turning up on time and hinted that he was busy with business. He spoke of his capers, his transcontinental travels and schedules he had to keep up with and all there was to in a social conversation. Listening patiently, I had begun to wonder once again until I could not take it anymore, 'I have been waiting for you all these days... you said you would get me out of here in ten days... do you still remember?'

"Edward kept looking at me and then burst into a loud laugh. He commented, 'I was wondering how much more crap you would take before it would get on your nerves. Of course I remember... why on earth do you think I have come here?'

"Those words from Edward rekindled my dying flame of hope. At last, I could look forward to a life worth living. That night, for the first time it occurred to me, that I had been purchased by my master even though I was married to him for records. I wondered if Edward had bought me from him or had my so-called husband agreed to divorce me. Edward revealed that neither of the two possibilities was correct. The lure of power and the lust for money seemed bigger than my existence to my master. He had presented me to Edward in hope of having a greater alliance with his companies. However, if one tried to interpret it, I had been traded once again, only difference being that I was willing to be traded this time.

"Later that night as I lay awake and close to Edward, I felt thankful to the pimp and my master. That night for the first time, I wondered what would have happened of me if I had remained in Kabul. Even though I could never forget the manner in which I had been exploited in the past two years, I did not wish to hold those men in contempt anymore; I had forgiven them all.

"I wished to make new beginnings devoid of hatred, terror, and tears, one last wish that kept nudging me from time to time – I should visit my home one last time before I left the continent for good. I wanted to visit my father's grave, amend the circumstance of my parting with my mother and if fate was too generous on me, meet my brothers. I hesitantly shared this with Edward. He was not anticipating such a request from my end, but he understood well that I deserved a reunion with my family. He assured me that he would try his best and he did. I dreamed of returning to my home, two and a half years after I had stepped out of it. This time though, I decided to part with dignity and honour from my house."

In late 2003, Afghanistan was engulfed by a hurricane of radical thought and practice. Reasoning, for some reasons, had alienated itself from the radical *diktats* of its preachers and its practitioners of faith. They were convinced that the only way to lead a life was in the way they dictated or death was imminent. Once a beautiful nation that I had glimpsed in some of olden films, now stood massacred by its own people. With the Western nations trying hard to enter Afghanistan and re-establish what seemed order in the society to them, instead instigated the radicals further.

In all that chaos, Rosha nurtured a childlike desire to meet her parents. I was sure, that dream of hers would never have come true. I was sure because she was sitting in front of me and talking to me. Had she visited Kabul then, I would have never met her and the rest would not follow. As if Rosha's life so far was not intriguing enough, it was about to surprise me further.

❑❑❑

12

Homecoming to Goodbye

"Even though Edward had explained everything to me and continued to do so every time he would notice me quieten up suddenly or lose attention of whatever he was speaking to me; he had realised that uncertainty dominated my thoughts. We spent a few days together in the same hotel as we had when he was there the last time. Every day I would dread the thought of returning to that villa if my master was to change his mind for whatever reasons. Contemplation prevented me from responding to Edward the way I wanted and he must have expected it too. Fortunately he understood my frame of mind and until the day arrived, when I stepped onto the tarmac, leaving that cursed land for ever, I could not be assured enough that this would happen for real.

"Edward and I boarded my master's private jet, rapidly reducing the distance and time between home and me. The plane was actually en route to Paris, with three daughters of my master, who were travelling there for perfume and cosmetic shopping," clarified Rosha.

I assumed that it was hardly another hour or so from Paris to London, therefore the wealthy Arab must have extended his favour further for Edward. But, I kept my doubts and questions to myself and Rosha went on.

"All of them were elder to me by two-three years at least. With Edward accompanying me, they wondered how their father could tolerate one of his women in other man's company. They kept exchanging glances from time to time over the journey, and I could sense the questions in their eyes loud and clear. What really intrigued me about them was that being women themselves, they should have come forward and wished me good luck; instead, they stared at me as if I was a traitor of some sort. The privilege to own anything that they wished had turned them into prudish women, who could not even bear the thought of parting away with anything they owned even if it had outlived its use.

"Edward was seated in the front cabin, busy with his business papers. He had officially managed to free me out of my master's clutches by asking my master to divorce me. Even though my master explained to him that it was not necessary, he could have me anyways, Edward insisted that it should be done. Once the legalities were settled, Edward arranged my visa to the UK and was now travelling to Kabul with me.

I was so overtly grateful to him for all he had done so far and more that I would learn about after we landed in Kabul."

"Kabul?" I blurted out in surprise for my assumptions had failed totally. My expression also confused Rosha for a moment.

"Where else did you think my home was, officer?" she asked me.

"Don't get me wrong, but in that time and circumstance… I assumed you meant London as your home, I am sorry, please continue," I said to her and let her carry on.

"As our plane began to descend from mountains of clouds towards land, I got a glimpse of my homeland after such a long time. My eyes welled up as the aircraft kept drawing closer and closer to the ground and finally hit the tarmac declaring the end of my days of slavery.

"No sooner had we stepped out of the jet, Edward and I were received by security personnel that he had already arranged for. The security men escorted us to our bulletproof car that was waiting to take us around the city once I knew as my hometown. Our car was escorted by two other cars, one ahead of us, and the other one behind. The moment we were together in the car, I held Edward's hand in mine and thanked him for all he had done and was doing. He patted my hand and remarked, 'You have a destiny of a hero, I guess.' I wondered what he meant by that. After a moment, he continued, 'Do you remember you had left this country as a slave and today you have returned to it with honours extended to a state guest?'

"Indeed, I was feeling no less than a queen at that time. Even though I had led an expensive lifestyle back in Saudi Arabia, it was more due to my master's fancy rather than my needs, and what I was experiencing then in Kabul was because Edward had planned to the very last detail ensuring my visit to be most comfortable.

"As our cavalcade of SUV's drove from the airport into the city, the initial joy of returning home withered away with every passing sight I saw. The city wore the look of death. It seemed like a decaying body that had been refused a burial. The walls were scarred everywhere. Bullet-holes had as though pockmarked and destroyed the once beautiful face of the city.

"Men, who could earlier be seen puffing their *hookahs*, listening to songs on their pocket radios, were now seen passing messages over their wireless handsets, resting the other arm over their Kalashnikovs. Handsome young men had grown to look barbarous wielding their overgrown hair and beards. They glanced at our car as if they were ready to punish us with our lives for having entered their territory. I realised that security arrangement around us was not just necessary but inevitable.

"Edward seemed equally shocked, we both kept looking through the dark tinted windows as if we were eyes of the departed souls of those who lived there once upon a time and were mourning over the state of those who were still alive.

"I can barely remember seeing children devoid of any deformity. Time, circumstance and the undying will to survive had turned them into creatures of another world. One could see them running beside streets with used rocket launchers, playing hide-and-seek in and out of rotting combat tanks, few teenage boys were already imitating as future leaders of the Taliban. It felt as if Afghanistan had shifted to a planet of its own, where people did not scare away at the sight of guns, or by the sounds of exploding bombs and mines. They had come to accept violence and death, chucking away the thought of misery from their minds. With over three decades of battle that the land and its people had faced already, their tear glands had long dried up weeping the loss of hundreds in the past.

"I could just not come to terms with the sight of the streets that I would take daily to my school and back home. It had all turned into a continuous heap of rubble. I had barely returned home and was already getting anxious to leave. As we steered through a few more lanes of distress, disaster and shattered homes, our car drew to a halt. In front of me stood the wounded and battered structure of what I had once grown up in and considered home. It seemed as if it had waited for that day, as though gasping for breath and borrowing life till I would visit it one last time so that it would happily collapse to its death after that.

"As I walked through the courtyard that once was a sprawling lawn filled with flowers of various kinds was now filled with tombs of many unknown. I shuddered at the sight. A sudden chill ran down my spine as I wondered if my mother rested beneath one of those graves too. Edward stood at a short distance from me. He had offered me the space I needed to be with myself. I wondered whom could I speak to find out about my family, when two security guards hurried to get me while the other two got Edward into the car.

"One of our guards had noticed some movement around the house, therefore, the commotion. Two of them stepped ahead to make sure wielding their pistols. A few minutes later, they escorted a woman wearing a *hijaab*. She must have been old I guessed as she took a while to walk to the car. I stepped out and walked towards her. She saw me through her veil and let out a loud wail before putting her arms across me. I recognised her to be our maid Zeba.

"The guards distanced themselves from us and Zeba moaned about what life had come to be. She revealed the tragic death of my mother. She was stoned to death for being a wife of a traitor. She was refused a burial in the usual burial ground so hers was the first grave in our courtyard and all the rest that lay there were such traitors that were not even worthy of an accustomed burial.

"My fears had indeed come true. My father, who had united our people, became their spokesperson to the world, he had devoted himself towards making sure that our countrymen do not bow down to the Russian rule… a man of such integrity was finally assassinated for encouraging people to send their children to schools and not to training camps of the Taliban. My mother was a devout wife and a pillar of support to my father in all his endeavours, yet she was stoned to death for being the wife of a traitor. Somehow, a thought still defeats my understanding that how could the Taliban then take my brothers with them. After all, how could anyone be trusted in a family of traitors?

"Zeba's son was her support and they still lived in the quarters that they used to while we were there. Her husband, who worked as a help to my father was absconding for the past six months after he had managed to avenge my father's murder. Only thing that had kept Zeba and her son from being killed was her father who was a preacher at a nearby mosque and a supporter of the Taliban.

"I had never heard about so much bloodshed in my life so far that I did in those twenty minutes or so. I was so pained by everything that I had no courage to enquire about my brothers. My mind grappled hope on one hand and fear on another as I finally enquired about them.

"My younger brother had been brainwashed and sent to fight in Iraq where some say that he met his end; as for my youngest brother, he lay next to my mother's grave, just like in life he always clung to her and it was so in death too.

"As I walked to their graves and knelt down, I realised that I was so shocked that I did not have a teardrop fall out of my eyes. I was shocked, angry, and disgusted. What had we done to deserve this I asked Zeba, who stood beside me. She stood silent. She did not have any answer to that question. She remained silent for a few moments more before she asked me a question instead. 'Why are you so ashamed to mention about Aashna, now that you have enquired about everyone else?' Her words shook me. Indeed, I had forgotten her. Why so, I wondered as I replied to Zeba, 'The last I saw of her was at the airport when we parted to our respective destinations.'

"Zeba had a steely look in her eyes as she pointed in the opposite direction to a grave that looked older than all others did. 'There she is,' she said pointing at her grave as her tears kept flowing as she walked to her grave. I had lost the energy to move, I wished to reason no more. From that moment on, I lost the fear of death myself. My sister, as I had mentioned earlier was not very resilient. It seems Aashna had managed to tear open the guts of her master. After her legal execution, her body was sent back home."

"The clergymen and self-appointed guardians of faith took that opportunity to show everybody that Aashna had sinned therefore met such an end. She had sinned because she was parented by a father who liked and supported the West and a mother who supported her husband's will. Thus, the whole family had earned shame and disgust of the community.

"A *fatwa*, meaning a religious summons was issued to my mother that she adhere to the laws of *Sharia* immediately or imagine the worst. She chose to die than surrender. One last time I looked at everything that lay before me. My house, the graves of my family, Zeba and the steel grey ambience that added to the sordid feelings I was to take away with me. There was no way I could possibly visit my father's grave as it was in that part of town, which was under the total control of the hardliners. I parted once again from my home that time for ever with memories of the barbarous and heinous manner in which my family had been reduced to dust. As I walked towards the car, I realised that no nightmare could make me shudder anymore after what I had seen with my eyes wide open. Alas, my dream of perfect farewell remained a dream. A goodbye that was not meant to be…"

❑❑❑

13

A Heartfelt but Wordless Condolence

Paying sincere and heartfelt condolence can be a mammoth task at times. This I realised after hearing to what Rosha had just revealed. I felt sorry for her and my feelings towards her loss were sincere. I wondered why words were failing me. Such words that could exactly describe how I felt for Rosha had as if vanished from my memory. How should I react I wondered. Comments such as – "It must have been very hard on you... you must have been heartbroken, devastated," did not even cross my mind, let alone saying one of them to this young girl, who sat facing me.

Since millenniums, humankind has been trying to establish the ideal way to live in peace and harmony. On the way to discovering a solution to the same, millions have lost their lives some for worthy reasons and many for not so worthy reasons. The loss of Rosha's entire kin had hardened her to such an extent that she could narrate the loss of her whole family, without a teardrop welling up in her eyes. Rosha did not deserve formality, and I was the last person to offer my condolence by quoting one of the usual lines meant for it and used a million times before.

"Rosha, I really desire to tell you what my heart feels but words… those appropriate words seem to have escaped. Your father battled for the liberty of his people and then to liberate their minds. Your mother battled for the rights of liberty your father stood for. Your sister battled to retain her liberty and right to live with dignity. Your brothers tried their best too. You too did not miss an opportunity to rescue yourself. It is very tragic when such heroic lives have to end in dishonour rather than glorification. Edward was absolutely correct when he told you that you had a fate of a hero. I think your whole family shared a common fate and I hope you end up achieving all that your family lived and died for. I apologise but I am unable to comfort you in any way in this moment of grief."

Rosha looked at me, patted my hand and said, "Officer, don't bother, all this happened six-seven years back. I had gotten over it long ago. Somewhere I must have been very foolish to believe that I would find my folks alive two years after my father had died in front of my eyes. That evening before heading back to the airport, I wondered what was the need for all that trouble. Was it hard to imagine that nothing would have remained? Was it surprising to learn that none of my family was living anymore? Afghanistan had transformed into a nation of people that believed in the survival of the clan, not an individual. There was nobody that had escaped the loss of his or her loved ones thus my loss did not seem special for any reason, but for one fact that my father had once saved the very same clan that had now razed his complete lineage. I asked myself if I was still that fourteen-year-old child hoping to bond with my mother or had I turned a temptress who could have her way with her new master.

"Then at times, I think why Edward had to go out of the way to take me to Kabul. He could have plainly refused, and what would I have done? At least I would have lived with a hope that my family was still breathing as me. Next moment I would comfort myself with the thought that it was better for me to have known facts earlier rather than nurse a desire that would have never come true in future.

"That afternoon when I departed from my home, I knew I was never to return there alive. Only in my thoughts, I could wander in what was once a garden, with fresh blossoming flowers and an air that carried its sweet fragrance, inviting birds and butterflies alike. The plants in that garden seemed to have disappeared into hibernation. Before I stepped into the car, I put my purse in Zeba's hand and asked her if she could do me a favour. Her tears were unstoppable. She knew ours was possibly the last farewell she would experience with living person. She just nodded her head signalling she would do anything I asked. I told her to plant a rose bush on every grave, as it did not need much care once it began to grow. Whenever a rose would bloom, it would remind her of me and she could console herself with the thought that at least one of them was hale and hearty in a faraway land.

"Whatever tears my eyes could produce, I emptied them all that day when I parted with Zeba. It was painful indeed but then I had survived it."

"Are you very fond of roses?" I questioned Rosha, trying to cut the tearful parting short.

"I like all flowers but roses are special to me as that's what my name stands for – a blooming rose."

Indeed, I said to myself, which other flower on this earth has the might of blooming over a stem of a thousand thorns except for the rose. The law abiding and disciplined officer in me had started melting away. I was starting to question the raw deal life had offered to such an angel. Somehow, I gathered myself at that and held back as there was more to find and I did not want to end up being hasty with my judgement.

I asked Rosha, "So did you hear from Zeba after that?"

"Officer, I did not know, where life would take me from there; and as for Zeba, she had no means to do so. That evening as the aircraft raced to take off, I realised that I had left behind that nubile Rosha in her house somewhere next to the graves of her family. Who travelled on that plane was a person who had decided to find answers to the questions that Rosha's life of sixteen years had put before me. I had somewhere decided to get to the roots of it all.

"I also could not forget that beside me sat an individual who had supported me so far because he liked me. How long was I going to remain his muse and how far would he fancy my eccentricities, was a question that only time could answer."

As Rosha commenced her journey to a new world with new aspirations, challenges and new fears, our journey came to an abrupt halt. A long queue of impatient vehicles stood before us. Our driver stepped out to check and I turned to look at the time. It was half past midnight. We had plenty of time left for the final formalities to complete at the airport, but we had very little distance left. Rarely though, traffic jams could sometimes turn out to be a blessing in disguise. I thanked all the elements of Nature to grant us the much-needed time. I had to take refuge in one more cigarette to prepare myself for what was to follow. Even today, when I light one, late at night, standing under the moonlit sky I remember that night. Sometimes, I light one just for that.

❑❑❑

14

Welcome to the New World

A multi-axle trailer had turned turtle, tearing the tanker open. Crude oil had spattered the moonlit silver asphalt with dark stains randomly. When I learned the reason of our unscheduled halt, I knew it was going to be a while before we could get going again.

As I dropped my cigarette to extinguish it, I noticed the thick black layer of oil seeping down slope towards us. Slow but steady it was edging its way towards our car. For a moment, it reminded me of the vicious Arab owner of Rosha. He dug oil for a living and here it was, that very same oil slithering like a monster, moving closer by the minute to devour Rosha.

Like a shooting star, a thought crossed my mind in a flash – Was this a sign of sorts to sense? Was I going to be responsible in turning Rosha's life into hell once again? I knew the answer to my questions, but conscience and law do not seem to complement each other always. I had a job to do, rest I could deal with as a professional hazard.

Rosha had stepped out of the car and was enjoying the midnight chill.

"Just look at her," I said to me, "Why can't you do something for her? If you wish, you could stop her from being doomed."

Only if I had known her a few weeks before, I would have been able to, but now it was too late. My helplessness angered me so much that I shot a question at Rosha, "Why did you have to come here at all when Edward had taken you to England?"

"That does not matter. Now that I have tried my best to achieve all that I wanted to and having failed at it, I won't hold you responsible for it, officer. You are not a villain; in fact, I think you would be the last humane person that would remain in my memory from now until the time I am put to rest," answered Rosha calmly, settling on a rock nearby.

The calm on her face, her surrender to the unknown, haunted me. I wanted to find a way out for her while she remained unperturbed by all that was happening around her. I wondered where she learnt to remain calm in situations that were a matter of life and death. Rosha's calm in those circumstances was a quality worth learning from her, while it disturbed my thoughts that were skimming through various possibilities that could help me come up with a valid reason to delay her deportation for now. The question nagging me was how I was going to do that. The possible solutions reeling in my mind needed to match with a perfect situation or incidence from Rosha's life.

Therefore, I asked Rosha, "Tell me what life has offered you after you left Afghanistan," and lit another cigarette.

"Why do you want to know?" she questioned back.

"One, because probably it would help me find some miraculous clue that could prove helpful, valid enough and you could be saved from the misery of deportation, and two, because it's a better way to kill time," I replied taking a drag.

Rosha smiled faintly as she nudged a question at me, "Oh! In that case, why don't you tell me a little about yourself, officer? That could kill time too."

"I can't do that, I am on duty," I said almost immediately. I knew it was a clumsy reply and we both burst into a laugh.

"Seriously, Rosha, tell me what happened, what England was like? Why did Edward leave you? What went wrong?"

"Officer, it is in fact the other way round. Before anything could go wrong, I decided to leave, besides I had other reasons too. You know when we left Kabul, I was completely shattered. I had lost everything that I once belonged to, all that was left to me was Edward, who kept supporting me throughout our flight to London. 'Life tests the mighty by throwing them into severe circumstances,' Edward had said to me on that plane. 'You have survived so far; that proves that you are meant to go on in life and make it worthwhile.'

"His words encouraged me and gave me the feeling of security that I needed at that time. I wondered how his family was going to react towards me, would they accept me, would his father be aware of my past, was I walking into another trap already. All sorts of questions ran through my mind on that flight and all Edward kept telling me was that he had arranged everything for me. I did not need to worry or feel scared of anything.

'Why are you doing this, Edward?' 'Simple, I love you; I want you to have what you deserve.' 'You know who I was and yet…' 'That was not a life you chose; it was brought upon you. Therefore, you do not need to feel guilty about it. Leave it behind and think about what you wish to do with the life that awaits you.'

"On that flight, Edward comforted me to no end, we hardly slept and as time passed by and the sky began to turn crimson, I knew we were close. Sunrise was going to bring in a new life for me from that day on. We landed at Heathrow early morning and I had taken my first steps on the land that was going to transform me for ever.

"Officer, when I had first travelled with my Arab master to his land, I knew I had surrendered myself to slavery even though he projected me to be his lawful wife. On the other hand, Edward had somewhat charted out a blueprint of a life that would be mine – being an aristocrat has its own benefits; therefore my purpose of stay in England was going to be as a foreign student.

"I could not believe it myself for a few moments. After all, it was quite a big leap from being a sex-slave to a student. Being freed from the shackles of bondage does not make one jubilant at once. It takes time for that person to gather himself. It is not easy to start thinking about yourself because as a slave you have to put your mind to accomplish your master's command. I had become a mere instrument that had stopped considering its own plight. Then all of a sudden, I had to come to terms with freedom, take charge of myself and once again ask myself what I desired in life, from life.

"That morning when we drove out of the airport, I confessed to Edward that I needed some time to decide how I was going to move forward from now on as I had lost touch with myself for quite some time. He was amused at my statement. 'Did you think that I was driving you to the university already?' he said.

"Officer, life was no more a mirage of hope for me; it had turned into a beautiful reality wherein I could foresee myself bloom into a fresh, beautiful rose and spread its sweet fragrance all around." Rosha turned silent to look at the heavy-duty cranes that were put into force to clear the overturned tanker.

Two tall arms of those mighty cranes raised the mammoth tanker from the ground and turned synchronously to place it away and out of the driving lanes of the highway. It was a sight to be seen. I was watching it and wondering what if one of the ropes coiled around the trailer were to snap. How many people would lose their lives just for being impatient and moving so close to the accident area?

While Rosha on the other hand related the scene by saying, "I was just like that immobile trailer, when two arms of fate lifted me and shunted me to an area where no one would cause any disturbance and neither would I to anyone else."

It seemed quite symbolic indeed, I thought to myself. Rosha had transformed herself into a machine like object while serving her rightful owner. Just like machines, she was devoid of her will, aspirations, and emotions. Her sole purpose of existence was to serve her master selflessly and as long as he wanted.

Just like the trailer on the road, destiny had turned her over probably to shake her back to life thus the arms of fate had helped shunt her to an area where she could be repaired, remodelled, and readied to steer her life the way she wanted. Nothing seemed to be an obstacle so far to me.

As there were more people anxious to know why Edward had turned head over heels for a girl from Afghanistan, now that she was coming to England with him could well seem like an arena where Rosha would have to fight her first battle. With only one supporter to cheer as against a stadium full to boo, it must have been a daunting task and I was eager to know how she managed that.

❑❑❑

15

Enchantment all the way!

Well aware of the fact that Rosha could understand Hindustani, I still confirmed, "You follow Indian poetry?"

"Yes, I do, officer."

"I am reminded of a couplet befitting your life so far and written by a woman poet *'Jab bhi milti hai mujhe, ajnabi lagti kyon hai? Zindagi roz naye rang badalti kyon hai?'* (She seems a stranger, every time I meet her. I wonder why life changes her guise so often.)"

Rosha smiled as she uttered, "Umrao Jaan Ada… Officer, have you read her works?"

"No, I have seen a film that was based on her life, why?"

"If you read her works, you would realise how profound her thoughts were and how simply she had managed to weave those beads of wisdom into a necklace of verse. She was no less than a saint.

"I had the opportunity to study many women of her kind and every time I finished with one more, I would wonder for days that those women had such introspective feelings, thoughts on life, humanity and so on and yet they were more glorified as prostitutes or women that lived on the outer edge of our societies. Look at Meerabai, for instance. Even she was abandoned by her husband, as he could not bear her celestial love for Krishna. Those women were no less than saints in their own respect. Yet very few or none was accorded the respect and honour they deserved while they were alive. It might seem intriguingly brutal to learn that seldom has the world acknowledged those that deserve to be."

"At this moment Rosha, you intrigue me to no end. I mean that if I understand everything correctly, you were born in 1986. You must have studied up to your secondary school before you moved to the Middle East. By the time, you were free and in England, it must have been the spring of 2003. Today we are at the end of 2008 so that makes you a young girl of twenty-two if I am right. Out of which you have spent year and a half here."

"Yes," replied Rosha wondering what my next question would be.

"What astonishes me is that you have managed to achieve so much in so little time."

"It's not impossible, officer."

"Indeed but it deserves a very strong drive, motive and what could have been yours I wonder. With Edward playing host this time, I was expecting you to be busy hobnobbing with the aristocratic gentry, living in palatial mansions, having a whirlwind romantic adventure on some yacht moored in Monte Carlo or an equivalent playground of the rich and famous."

"All that happened too officer, but then I had been granted the privilege to grow beyond being labelled the 'Girl of the season'. While Edward had me an apartment in the city, very close to where he lived, even though we spent a lot of time together, we lived in separate homes. He was very careful about his reputation, and did not want me to be taken for granted as one of his indulgences.

"To make matters worse for me, Edward did not tell me anything much about his family even after I had asked him about it on various occasions. Later I realised that he did not wish to burden me with the additional pressure of grooming myself to the expectations of his parents and others close to him. He would remind me of the first time he saw me. I had caught his attention. It wasn't my display of etiquettes, or charm. It was just plain me. He would often quote, 'I could see a diamond while others dismissed you as a rock.' Indeed officer, he did spot me, he did put me into a process that brought about the cut, carat, and colour into me, and people were amazed whenever they saw me accompanying Edward to select few places, where he was very sure that no one would try any stunts to embarrass me.

"London was a different world altogether. It was as though the picture postcards my father showed us often had turned real. The Westminster Abbey, the London Bridge, the Bloody Tower, the Buckingham Palace all stood their ground majestically, while I wandered through them like an enamoured fan that turns speechless when faced with the star she desires to meet the most. The glittering skyline of London through the Eye of London was a breathtaking view that transported me into a different space altogether. From the height one is at, it is not very hard to imagine that stars have had a change of heart thus leaving the smoky sky, had decided to spread their glitter from the earth to beyond. The more I saw, more it occurred to me that Edward was not introducing me to his family. Even though it bothered me, but what do you expect from a sixteen-year-old girl? Temptations kept my worries at bay for the time being, until one day when all my worries got the better of me.

"One fine morning, Edward woke me up and planned to take me on a drive to the countryside. I showered, wore a light floral dress that suited the trip and the bright sun, which I was beginning to learn, was not a usual fare. The countryside of London reminded me of pastel sketches we would make as kids sitting on some hill close to home, with my father relaxing under the shade of a tree nearby, reading one of his favourite authors and my brothers would prepare their kite for the launch, while mother would busy herself with Zeba to serve us some sandwiches and *sherbet*. Our drawings back then did not capture the reality of Nature exactly; it was more of a combination of what we saw and how good we could draw.

"Those blunt hillocks with shades of green pastures covering them, a brook that might appear from nowhere and disappear as suddenly, those small cosy cottages with smoking chimneys, all so beautiful and pleasant to the eyes. The soothing morning sun had just begun to rise higher when Edward decided to retract the hood of his convertible. I enjoyed watching the black hood wiping the blue sky away. A little later, as I turned to see out of the window, I noticed a very ancient monument like mansion that stood by itself as if prudish of its solitude.

"The structure must have eroded over centuries but that very eroded skin had brought out a gold feel to its bricks as they shone under the top sun. With a generous spread of gardens and boundaries marked with shapely hedges, it proved that the place still had people living in it or at least taking care of it. I casually enquired about the place with Edward and he wondered if I liked it. Of course, I had liked it and wanted to visit it too, only if it were that easy. Edward did not say a word as from the next bend he turned his car into a lane which kept bringing us closer and closer to that mansion, and no matter how I rephrased my questions to Edward about the mansion, and if he knew its owners or were they relatives, he just kept driving towards it, and then through its regal iron gates and onto the porch, where he chivalrously stepped out and opened the door for me. 'Welcome Miss Rosha, you have arrived finally and I am delighted to introduce you to my parents!' Then turning his arm to me, exclaimed, 'May I guide you Miss?' I literally froze at the spot. I mean I was not even dressed for the visit. Then that was Edward's style of handling things. Just when you expected nothing more than the usual, he would sweep away the earth below you. He had done something very similar when I had accompanied him to the airport to see him off. That day at Edward's family-home, the feeling was no different.

"You know when I met Edward's parents for the first time, they were as nervous as I was. While they wondered, what this Afghani girl was all about, I wondered how I was supposed to present myself to them. As I took my first steps towards the door, Edward comforted me by telling me that I would be fine, and that there was nothing to worry about. As I walked through the tall corridor of that mansion I saw for myself for the first time, what aristocracy truly meant. Walls were adorned with classical paintings, plaques and honours bestowed on the family over generations, elaborate portraits of the ancestors posing proudly in their military finery, showing off their chest full of gallantry medals. Few pictures of the present family hinted at the fact that Edward was the only child. Walking through that corridor was no less than a personal museum of sorts and beautiful flower arrangements that offered a very pleasant air to the overall ambience.

"I was headed to a huge, well-crafted wooden door that Edward opened effortlessly, giving me a glimpse of what lay beyond. What caught my eye was the twinkling light of a massive chandelier and as my eyes tilted lower, I saw a beautiful woman in her fifties waiting to welcome me. My heart skipped a beat as I took the next step and walked through that door. It was dreamlike in a way for me. It was as though I had crossed over into another world where I would be loved, cared for, given all the opportunities that I had lost for no reason. Crossing that door had turned me into something similar to 'Alice in Wonderland'. The manner in which Lady Elizabeth, Edward's mother and Lord Andrew, his father put me to ease, I felt as if we had known each other for years and were catching up after a long time.

"I would be lying if I said that I wasn't enamoured by the grandeur as well as the shining blue sapphire guarded by small soldier-like diamonds that adorned Lady Elizabeth's neck. Not to say that my earlier master was not comparable, but I was blinded to all the glitter he owned. Now for the first time my eyes were beginning to see all that lay before them. I was beginning to think that finally I had been awarded justice, after all the atrocities I was put through.

"Meeting Edward's parents meant a necessary formality for Edward, it meant a kind of formal approval and acceptance for me and as for the parents, they seemed slightly nervous, slightly intrigued and very anxious to know me as I was the one Edward had chosen over all other women.

"Lady Elizabeth seemed very motherly and concerned; I could see that she got more worried with every incident of my life that I shared with her. Lord Andrew sympathised with me over my plight and then encouraged me to start afresh now that I was under their guardianship. I had suddenly found a family that I had lost years ago, I thought. I was happy and relieved until Lady Elizabeth revealed her fears in a direct question, 'What do you aim to do in England, my dear?' 'Edward wants me to go to college,' I replied almost immediately. 'Oh! So looks like you want to fulfil all that he desires from you,' she remarked.

'I think Edward feels that it would help me stand on my own feet some day, besides I could never have imagined such kind of generosity from anyone after all that I had been through,' I replied clarifying my stand.

'Have you thought over what stream of education would you like to pursue, my dear?' questioned Lord Andrew. 'I am sorry sir, but I haven't found the time to think about it so far,' I replied, realising that I had been in England for a good fifteen days by then and this thought had not crossed my mind even once. Lord Andrew walked up to me, stroked his palm on my head gently, in a fatherly way, and said, 'Listen child, listen to me carefully as I don't like to repeat myself often. Fate has given you an opportunity to transform a wasteland into a blossoming garden. Therefore don't let this chance slip out of your hands. We would be proud to see you succeed and so would Edward, isn't that all he brought you here for?'

"That final question from Lord Andrew clarified everything that they wished to tell me. With a shower of sympathy over my past, a nourishing promise of support for my future and the seemingly painless trimming of my dreams of loving Edward all my life, I knew the boundaries of the liberty I had been granted amongst the people I was beginning to consider my family in the land that I had accepted to be my home.

"Today when I look back at those days I realise that the poor Lord and Lady had a legacy to protect, how could they have their only son stray away and alter their bloodline for ever?

"So that is how your meeting with Edward's parents ended," I questioned.

"No, not at all, officer. The British have not managed to rule almost all over the globe just like that. They have honed their skills of diplomacy over centuries of practice; don't you know that already, officer?" she replied.

Indeed, they had, I said to myself. What they had once practised to rule over their colonies, today they were using that very same tact to protect and govern their families. That meeting must have concluded with more encouraging and inspiring statements from the two, which I did not want to hear nor confirm from Rosha. What mattered was what made her stay put in such surroundings for a good four years or so.

I still wasn't able to find a way out for her, when I heard an almost synchronic hum as the sleepy engines revved up to life. The wheels began to rotate gradually. Exhausts puffed a cloud of smoke, I knew the jam was over and with it came an end to our borrowed time. We were back in our seats and heading to our destination. There was very little time and distance left for any more miracles. Rosha had surrendered herself to fate and I was bound by duty. No matter what our trappings were, an unfinished story always leaves behind questions. Finding answers to those questions only gives rise to some more questions and one has to satisfy oneself with assumptions that suits one's taste best.

I did not need to assume anything while the storyteller was still in front of me. Perhaps if we had a little more time on hand, this thought would not have entered my mind. It wasn't that I was the only one worried about it; even Rosha sensed that we were closing in to the airport with every passing minute, and we had lost the luxury of spending a few moments in silence to relish and digest the memories just shared. Rosha was not bothered about where her life was heading nor would she be able to tell me all that I wanted to know. She had calm on her face that reflected through her eyes too. She remained that ways for some time and I did not disturb.

❑❑❑

16

In the Realm of Knowledge

We both remained silent for some time, kept looking at the lane-stripes shooting away at high speed. It reminded me of the distance we had covered in terms of kilometres and how many more were ahead, before we would arrive. But, what about the distance that I had covered in terms of time?

Rosha and I had encompassed her childhood, her life as a concubine and now, once again she was at the crossroads of her life. This time though, she had all the aids at her disposal. All she had to do was choose the road and decide to walk.

I don't know why, words just came to my mind, out of my mouth, that ended our interval of silence.

"Rosha, you have come a long way in life and I am sure nothing can stop you from achieving all that you wish," I said to her.

"For a while even I had begun to think that ways, only to realise later that it takes a lot of people and a lot of things to work in your favour to make that line come true," replied Rosha nonchalantly.

"You sound as though you had given up long ago in life," I prodded her.

"Bit by bit hope escaped me and I was left with this one last chance, which has escaped me too," Rosha replied and travelled back into her world of past.

"It was not easy for a girl like me to decide what I really wanted to do in life. That in addition, when the question was put to me by Edward's parents, it only doubled the pressure on me. I had to decide to do whatever I would like to. But what was that I really liked? What was that I necessarily should have done? I just kept going in circles; even Edward sensed my quandary.

"When I told Edward about the soft manner, in which his parents had warned me to stay in limits with him, Edward would only draw me closer, and whisper in his warm breath into my ear, 'Make yourself worthwhile, shine like a star, blossom into a person that people would be proud to accept you as one of their own. I know you have it in you.' Those warm and encouraging words from Edward would make me melt away in his arms. Even if I wanted to keep distance, I could not help surrender myself to the one man that I had lost my heart to. Waves of passion and bliss would wash away those worrisome questions from my mind for the time being.

"Every morning I would wake up before Edward. I lay next to him, and wondered that if I carried on the way I was how long I would be able to keep Edward interested in me. He did not just expect passionate sex from me. He wanted to make me a graceful young woman who would have no shortcomings that could prevent her from being considered an able match he could marry in time to come. I kept waking up to such thoughts most of the mornings. It felt like a bad hangover, a price one had to pay for the great night spent.

"One such morning, I did not wake up; instead, I slipped into deep sleep when a dream transported me through a dark tunnel of time. On the other end, I was awaited by the visuals of my life that had gone by. They swept past my eyes and kept repeating themselves like the horses of a carousel in the carnival of life. Good memories were the white horses and the bad ones were black. They kept going up and down and the carousel continued to rotate, until I could sense a pattern in them – a larger picture.

"When I finally woke up, it was noon. Edward had left long ago and I was fortunately left to myself to deal with the afterthoughts of what I had finished watching with my eyes closed. I had realised one thing for sure that my life had turned into a nightmare not because my father was dead, but because he was crucified for not adhering to the *diktats* of faith leaders who wished to restructure and reinterpret the beliefs of the followers by might and fear.

"My whole family dissolved into dust because my father stood his ground until those custodians of faith found it easy to kill him rather than reason with him. The fear of death can command plentiful to surrender and in this case, my father's murder equalled that of a self-proclaimed *sultan*. Therefore, his murder would benefit the conspirers in more than one ways. It would put the rebellious men to ease as they would realise that my father's fate could well be theirs too, and they would join in willingly or unwillingly with the rest, who in any case moved in herds and walked to wherever they were herded to.

"The masses desire a leader. Sometimes they choose one and at times, they have to surrender to one. They don't rise to become one themselves. It is one amongst them, who has faith in his thinking, capacity to see a larger picture and reasons with others to think like him. Such men are unfortunately too little or rare, so when a group loses one of such men, they find no other option but to surrender to the new regime. In this case, the new regime called for unquestioned belief and practice of the reinterpreted faith too.

"Indeed faith is unquestionable. However, until a belief transforms into one's faith, it has to encounter a severe attack of doubts, questions, reasons, etc, to prove its influence and strength. A dispute of faith had desecrated not only my home but also my homeland. On the one hand, it allowed murdering people such as my father and on the other hand, it permitted trading innocent children to serve men well beyond their father's age too.

"Faith had caused a great amount of turmoil in my life and to me faith in God meant an invisible source of energy that flowed through everything and everywhere. I did not need to remind myself of it five times a day that God existed and that I necessarily needed to be thankful to him always. My father had introduced the concept of God in such a way that without compulsively remembering him, God would always remain in our conscience and help us do the right thing.

"As for the clerics and the fundamentalists, this kind of education meant clear and present danger. If they did not act immediately, then others would question the existence of their faith too in time. If a faith is so weak that a humble man like my father could challenge its merits, then I rather accept that that faith was more of a hoax that would benefit its propagators and would devour its followers when the rest of the world would wake up to its fury.

"Such thoughts consumed my mind that day and when Edward finally arrived that evening, I told him that I had made up my mind about what I wanted to do in life. I told him that I wanted to study religion, its birth, its need, its purpose, all kinds of them that existed and those that had perished with time. I wanted to try understanding the real reasons of having gone miserably off-course to have turned barbaric against our own kind. For the first time, that day I learnt that such stream of education was called 'Theology' and that was what I had decided to put myself to study.

"Edward was surprised with my choice. Looking into his questioning eyes, I still remember walking close to him as we settled onto a couch, together. 'It wasn't just a person who killed my father. It was his faith that drove him to do so. Therefore, I need to learn about where faith gets its strength from, how it transformed one neighbour into a murderer of another, converted a beautiful country into an endless graveyard and the land of half dead people wandering around. If this is what faith can do, then do we need one at all?' I just summed up the best way I could.

"Edward kissed me tenderly and complimented, 'You had this wondrous aura around you that attracted me the first time I saw you, and that is the very same quality that keeps drawing me even closer with every passing day. I knew that you were not the type who would settle down for a compromise. I am glad you've made a choice that would help you deal with your demons, and help you build into a strong person from within.'

"With a man like Edward beside me and the free reign to study, I could not have asked more from life at that time. I could just be grateful. Although one thought kept making me regretful from time to time – had my father been alive, he would have been very proud of me. On the other hand, it would make me wonder that if he were to be alive, would I have chosen to do what I had?

"Within a few weeks from then on along with regular preparatory tutorials at home, I found myself walking through the majestic corridors of my college trying to find my class. It was a great feeling. Even though I wasn't older than the rest that attended college, I felt elder to them in experience. While they were more interested to find out who was going out with whom and who was the one loaded enough to take care of their whims and fancies, I was engrossed in learning about those men, who had lived centuries ago and had sensed the inevitable need to reason the existence of mankind and the manner in which it may flourish.

"The oratory skills of my professors would transport me into a world and time that does not exist anymore. The kind of people and thoughts they discussed don't seem to find any place in our today's world. Sheer amazement kept making me learn more and more of how man began to think beyond himself and of things that did not seem to exist yet gave ample evidence of its existence. I realised that there is an unaccountable toil put in for centuries together by thinkers that did so to help answer their own questions and later, even better if it could help others solve their problems too. Their selflessness in doing so commanded reverence. Their farsightedness humbled me. Their sufferings made me forget mine and six months into that world had gotten me so engrossed in learning, I had almost forgotten that all this was possible due to Edward's magnanimity. Whenever I acknowledged him for it, he would say that I deserved it and not because he wanted me to do so."

Indeed, Rosha was destiny's own child in true sense, I said to myself. As she kept talking endlessly about her journey into the realm of wisdom, philosophy and the philosophers, I kept looking at her and wondered where did she begin from and how far she had travelled.

Rosha suddenly noticed that I was not listening to her as she questioned, "Officer, am I talking too much? Shall I stop?"

Her questions shrugged me out of my own thoughts as I said to her, "Not at all, I was in fact listening to your finds when I suddenly slipped into thinking about you. Just look at you, do you realise how much you have managed to gather at such a tender age? You must have put in years full of long days and sleepless nights, and in a matter of three hours you have almost been able to tell all that you stand for today. It seems strange, isn't it? I mean, it takes a lifetime to gather all the experiences, and it takes a few hours to filter them and choose those few that you wish to keep with you at all times."

"Officer, you are speaking more like a thinker now," said Rosha trying to lighten the mood and I played along.

"Why, anything wrong with that?" I questioned.

"No, I was just wondering whether officers on duty were permitted recreational thinking," said Rosha as she burst into a smile. I smiled too and kept looking at her.

Rosha was just a few hours away from uncertainty. With her Saudi passport and her deportation papers ready, there was very little or no chance of helping her out. But, at that moment, she was not bothered about what was going to follow. She was smiling away and enjoying those moments to their fullest. Some time ago, it was she who had said that she had lost all hope bit by bit. Was she contradicting herself, I wondered. No one besides Rosha could solve the puzzle, thus I shared it with her.

"Indeed I said that I had lost hope bit by bit and have no more left now. But that was not meant for me in person. I had lost hopes of doing what I had planned accomplish once. My aim of writing a book that could help me share my thoughts with countless people… reason through it a simpler way of thought, and my plans of further research… I have lost hopes of pursuing all that any further. Having said that, it does not mean that I have given up living already; as long as my breath remains loyal to my body and soul, I will continue to keep an account of my capers and setbacks.

"Officer, I am regretful about my incomplete work but I am not a bit resentful about it anymore. Who knows, probably the derivations I had drawn in time were meant to remain locked within me. Maybe time was playing its old trick once again. If I came out with my secrets, time would lose the importance it had found in today's world, our lives. If I were to say that, we are still grappling to find a way to live happily while we voluntarily ignore it.

"Man and his needs have grown so far and beyond that, he could keep reincarnating a few times at least to fulfil those unfulfilled desires of his first life. The unfulfilled desires are meant to remind us that we may not have been committed enough to deserve their accomplishment or maybe we needed to work harder or it was in the better interest of our future pursuits that we lose out on a few.

"In all this unnecessary chaos that man has created around himself, is today governed by time. If a certain thing is accomplished in a certain unit of time then it reflects into profits. Otherwise, it results in bankruptcy and unexplainable crash of the stock markets. Officer, don't you think that money is a more real universal faith than any others that we follow today?"

It had never occurred to me that ways but then I had no reason to oppose her claim too. "It's an interesting interpretation, I must say," I remarked and let her give me more insights.

"No matter which faith and its people battle whosoever, they both have one firm belief in common – Money. Nobody in the world questions its solidarity. While religions and its torchbearers have over the time arrived at a consensus that there is only one God, they still battle to seek popularity for the one they represent. But money, no one dares to dispute its shine, its sound, and the all-pervading power that can buy off anything in today's world. Who knows how far are we from a day when the world's computers might just decide to go berserk for an hour and humankind might just cease due to the chaos it would cause.

"We have found a new Lord Almighty and trained a new slave. The Lord – Money has bestowed us with the liberty to own all that we desire and the gizmos are there to do our work for us. In between these two, we just wish to sit and reap the benefits of it all after trading our estates of morality, ethics, and humanity because in the religion of money every grouse can be settled with money itself. There is no need for any sort of realisation or penance. All that one needs to do is pay up, and *walla*! No one has any complaints anymore.

"There was a time when I would entertain tearful todays for the loss of yesterdays but now I seem to have realised at least that much. It does not help you go back to that time to correct your follies. When the only direction we are left with is pointing forward, the only reason I look back at times is to remind me of the fault lines that I need to beware ahead. The regret is that one yet trips over a new one from time to time, the way I have now, once again and am here, paying a price for my ignorance. Since I can think this way, I am able to enjoy the present moment rather than sacrifice it to honour my regrets. I hope I have clarified myself well enough."

What could I say to Rosha? Her answers and the wisdom she had derived, had transformed her into a spring of fresh water that could never stagnate, no matter what obstacle tried to block her path, she would flow over or under it and make way to merge into the great ocean some day. Rosha was not the one to surrender before that and not the one to settle for anything less than that.

❑❑❑

17

A Candid Invitation

Rosha had mentioned about how important time had grown to be in our day-to-day lives a short while ago, and I was reminded of her words when I received a text message. "We have arrived. How long will you take?" was the question asked by one of my seniors via a text message.

I looked around and realised that we had already entered Mumbai and were just about passing by the RK Studios.

"Thirty minutes max," was my reply.

It was way past two in the morning and Rosha's flight would depart at five forty-five. There were not many formalities to be completed at the airport, but I could not take time for granted. I was surer of the thirty minutes now than the two and a half hours at the airport.

"Rosha, we are about to reach the airport and from what you have told me so far, life seemed to have taken an upbeat swing for you. I cannot think of what could go wrong there that you had to leave," I asked.

"Officer, let me tell you that I did not leave England wilfully. My departure was a sort of payback to Edward's family for all that they had done for me in those years that I lived there. They weren't bad people, but they had a legacy to maintain. No matter how much I excelled in whatever I did, I was applauded for my thinking, my opinions, and my writings, but was still considered an outsider. Their generosity had well-defined limits and it was for me to realise my limits for my own good.

"Officer, in the company of people that I moved with, whenever I escorted Edward, people never looked at me as his wife-to-be; instead, they would compliment Edward that he had an eye for women of class. No amount of etiquette and dressing in those western dresses was going to make me the princess that Edward deserved to marry.

"I had not forgotten my past in the Arabian sands. However, England had much more to offer and far more to lure. I scored very well in my first term and discovered that one of my professors knew Edward's family well. He was fond of me in a fatherly way and complimented Edward's family for being so benevolent to have given me the opportunity to learn. Edward's parents too were surprised at my single-minded dedication towards my education. Even though Lord Andrew had subtly warned me in the beginning itself, but my academic achievements were compelling them of having second thoughts about me. I was not too sure of it but Edward kept reminding me of it from time to time and I kept the flame of hope alive in me that someday, probably the unthinkable might just happen. Maybe the deserving person would get his due.

"My professors were confident of my progress because they were aware of the capacity of my understanding and the depth of my pain. They knew I had a reason to study what I had chosen. I was looking for the reason our family and country had suffered. The motive for the deaths of thousands of innocents and the answers to that were hidden somewhere in those tall aisles of the endless shelves of the library.

"With every passing day, I understood things better and started looking at everything in a different light. With knowledge seeping in, I was getting answers to questions that had remained questions until then. Later I found myself questioning my motive itself. I mean, I wanted to get to the root of the problem and find out why Afghanistan and its people had to suffer the way they had and are even today. This question was my motive or pursuit. Is it a motive enough – I would question myself sometimes. What would I do if I found an answer? Would anybody pay heed to my finds? Why would anyone even want to do so? Such kind of questions would distract me from time to time but I kept going. Whenever my own faith in me turned weak, I took support of my teachers' faith in my work. They motivated me to carry on without paying heed to any thought that disturbed me or derailed me from my current course. Thus, I kept surging ahead with tremendous speed and fewer stops of distraction.

"Time no more meant anything to me. A year had gone by and I had still not seen the other corner of my college. I had made friends. Most of them were kind; some seemed insecure, as I was quite a show stealer in class. Boys were obviously interested in having a romantic encounter with an exotic Asian girl. I was aware of all that surrounded me, but I was not open to any leisureliness then. I was in search of something bigger and more important. Not only did I have to find answers to my questions, but I also needed generous amount of time to regurgitate on them and then derive my own conclusions.

"Over the time, I had decided that I was going to make a name for myself, leave a mark behind to be remembered as this feisty girl who came out of nowhere and shared her humble finds that will remain as long as the world remains such. The only way I could do that was by writing, contributing my papers to various journals. I had started by writing about what I felt about life, humanity, and religion. These three are undisputedly interconnected in today's world.

"Somewhere and somehow, religions have grown bigger than those who realised them and preached their thoughts to everyone devoid of any distinctions. They did not do so for name; they did it for sharing their sight, their knowledge with plenty as that would help in spreading it further. Those selfless saints, seers were not the ones who sat down to scheme books that craftily bound man into a maze of fear. 'One wrong step could anger God. Thus, penance was inevitable.' Therefore a judge became an indispensable necessity, so the priests and priesthoods evolved and where would they practise their judgements, so churches, mosques, synagogues took shape and the money that was needed to get all this up and running, came from the kings, wealthy thieves, plunderers that had enough to throw provided they got an entry into the upper strata and were to be respected for their nobility and fairness.

"In all this congregation of the wealthy and the mighty few, where do you think did the common person surface? What did he have to contribute, so where does the question of recognition arise at all for the poor clueless common man? It took him centuries before he could understand what the looting, killing, and various other kinds of torture that humankind was put through was to create herds of followers that would not question the merits of the faith they might have been forced to accept and adhere.

"How many have the courage to choose death over life, so like herds humans divided themselves from time to time from faith to faith, mainly to secure their survival. These very men toiled and slaved to raise structures of faiths. Synagogues, chapels, and mosques were built to stand tall symbolising it as sacred places of worship, as a monument and symbol of peace. Tell me, officer, what could be a bigger paradox than this that too when one is aware about how religious prejudice has killed man more than all the epidemics and famines put together? Nevertheless, some supremely adamant people have not given up. They are still busy in raising the tower of their minaret taller than the canopy of the neighbouring synagogue. Does this please God? Is this why He gave us all brains that helped us hone incredible skills and above all a mind that distinguishes us from the beasts? In fact, that very mind showed us the way wherein one could depend totally on oneself. It could transform a prince like Siddhartha into Gautama Buddha and could drive a knowledgeable king like Ravana and most of his family to death due to his lust for Sita.

"All that one needs to be aware of is that there is a force that exists for one who wishes to believe in it. That does not mean that who do not sense its existence or feel the need to accept it, should be threatened to believe. This sham of fear has turned man into his own worst enemy, further more ignorant and insensitive as compared to our ancestors who lived in caves and made the first tools from chiselling stone.

"I guess when man left the cave, he left behind humanity there itself. With the discovery of tools and with it the concept of self-reliance must have made man worry only for his own needs. Assuming that all would do the same, make their own tool, everybody would be self-contained. Do we realise the magnitude of change it must have resulted into amongst humankind on discovery of one small tool? That spear or dagger or whatever that killing or hunting tool man had learnt to make, he had faith in its capability, so why don't we consider it the earliest religion man ever surrendered to? On the other hand, when man discovered a better tool, all shifted to the use of the new one. Obviously, for it must have proved more convenient and effective for the purpose as compared to its predecessor.

"If the same approach is applied to various religions, many have outlived their purpose, so why are we dragging their carcass around and trying to fool ourselves by believing that they are alive and still have immense, unexploited power in them? This is what I had come to think of in a year's time. I was motivated by my teachers to present a paper on what I considered my personal writings. It was published in one of the journals and I had tasted victory for the first time ever.

"Edward's joy knew no bounds when he learned about it. Each time we met, he found me edging forward to prove myself worthy of having been offered an opportunity to discover myself. Somewhere behind all my academics and my transforming personality, Edward was turning more certain of facing no objection from anybody when he would reveal his intentions of marrying me. He did not want his parents to be unhappy and pretend otherwise in public. Thus, he wished that a day should come when either of his parents should discuss this proposal with me in a manner traditionally prescribed.

"I could not believe my own eyes, when one day I saw Lady Elizabeth walking through the corridor of my college. Even though she was aptly dressed, royalty could not be ignored. As the heads turned to look where she was going, eyes widened when they saw her hug me tightly and plant a peck on my cheek, just like any caring mother would do to her child.

"We were meeting after a long gap. It wasn't that we had not met after our first meet but other meetings were nothing more than a brief chat at a party or at Royal Albert Hall, where Edward would take me to watch opera and often we would bump into his parents.

"However, that afternoon, Lady Elizabeth was there with an intention to meet me and invite me over to a family lunch the following Sunday. I could sense the purpose of such a meeting and the formal invitation, but I did not let excitement reflect on my face thus remained ardent and respectful to her, until I saw her drive away.

"That day joy was boundless for Edward and me. It was a victory of sorts for both of us. We tried to look at the time gone by, the decisions we made about anything and everything then. I had managed to impress people who could never imagine bending the rules of their tradition. We kept complimenting each other and kept making plans for our future together.

"A future that would wash away the bounds of racial divide, wherein two people would blend into one forgetting the religious prejudice and other divisions that divided humanity further into superior and inferior races. Somehow, it meant a new beginning for us in more ways than one. Edward was sure that his parents would never turn down his wish, if it were truly deserving of the honour. He, his faith in his own acumen and in his commitments to me had won that day. What we both awaited anxiously was to hear it from his parents once, so that contemplations could be put to rest for good."

❑❑❑

18

The Unforgettable Sunday

"Edward grew anxious with every passing day and wished that Sunday should dawn the very next day if it were possible. Ultimately, it dawned when it was supposed to and once again, we drove across that beautiful countryside. Once again, I enjoyed the picturesque drive to the house I had taken fancy to once in the past. Besides bright sun, everything seemed as before. A grey overcast sky had slightly dampened the colour of the fresh green pastures, but it also turned the overall atmosphere very romantic.

"Once again I walked through that regal corridor, but this time I looked at everything there a tad differently. After all, I was going to become the daughter-in-law of the family that would live here. It was going to be my house some day.

My heart raced faster and I wondered how many people, relatives of Edward's family awaited to meet me. Once again, Edward opened that grand old oak door and we entered inside to be welcomed by Edward's parents. Unlike what I had expected, it was strictly a family lunch, with just four of us. I assumed that this would be their way of discussing matrimony. Unlike in Afghanistan, where the bridegroom is accompanied with so many friends, relatives, and parents, that even the bride's family seems confused until one of the members from the boy's side points out which of the boys was the suitor.

"Lord Andrew seemed very impressed with my progress so far and although Lady Elizabeth was not the thinking type, she had read some of my works and she remarked – 'It compelled me to think about it.' We had been there for a good two hours and had discussed everything under the sun that one would discuss to make each other comfortable, before coming out with the main purpose of the meeting. I continued to oblige Lord Edward with my thoughtful answers to all that he asked me, while Lady Elizabeth enquired from Edward about all those weeks he had not showed up at the family gatherings and other social do, where his absence seemed rude. Edward apologised for it and relieved himself with one excuse or another.

"Edward was growing impatient to hear his father come out with the real purpose of that lunch meeting. Lord Andrew sensed his son's edginess well in time and asked Edward's permission to borrow me for a stroll. Edward obliged and I stepped into the sprawling garden with Lord Andrew, who, just like my father, introduced me to various blooming flowers as though it was necessary that I knew them by name, as they were no less than family to him. As he described each plant and flower specie, how difficult it was to get those to flourish in the unpredictable English weather, I began to feel at ease. I could sense that we would share a great rapport in future, as he reminded me of the mannerisms and likes very similar to my father.

"We had walked a few yards by then, with flourishing flowers brushing me softly. Lord Andrew took a while to find the right words and the right point in conversation to come out with the real stuff as he said that Edward had indeed proved himself an eligible bachelor. He had methodically gained the confidence of those who were once Lord Andrew's colleagues in his business and in time to come, Edward would seamlessly take over the entire show and run it as responsibly as Lord Andrew had for the past four decades.

"Since such men were hard to find, Edward was quite the boy any parent of equal or higher stature would desire to offer their daughter in marriage. Therefore, alliances from wealthy and respected families were frequent those days. We kept walking as he spoke of the alliances that they had considered for Edward already. With each prospective alliance he spoke of, I began to wonder whether Lord Andrew was trying to make me aware of the forthcoming loss they were going to bear by accepting me as their daughter-in-law or was he trying to tell me that if I were nursing such a dream, then I had better realise that dreams don't come true often.

"I had, by then, heard enough about the billions of dollars and pounds worth of business that would merge, and the kind of market shares their family would enjoy and all under the sun that they could rule if Edward were to marry this girl that belonged to such a family, or that one, whose family had inherited limitless amounts of wealth from the gold mines their forefathers owned in Africa. I was so exhausted listening to such probabilities that I hoped Lord Andrew would stop bragging about all those possibilities and attend to the one real option, realistically with a short and straight answer like, 'Yes' or 'No'. The way he went about discussing prospects it seemed that if it were permitted, Lord Andrew would marry off Edward to all those girls he had discussed so far. That banter had exhausted me so much that I said to Lord Andrew 'Sir, it might sound out of context, but even we belong to the royal family of Afghanistan. Our ancestors were traced to have had family ties with the Mughals too.'

"Lord Andrew stopped in his footsteps and turned to look at me, with not the slightest change in his expression. He said, 'Indeed, my dear. Up till your father, your claim stands merit; unfortunately the same cannot apply to you.' 'I am sorry sir, but doesn't it seem absurd?' 'It does but then fate happens to be a load of absurdity, which one has to drag along with all their lives. I did not wish to reveal facts that even your own father had kept from you, but the nature of present circumstance has left me no other option, Rosha.' While Lord Andrew turned silent as though to prepare himself to fire his final shot, my thoughts raced at lightning speed to figure out how on earth was he going to justify his claim.

'You are not the biological child of your parents, Rosha. In fact none of you were born to your mother. She could not have children,' said Lord Andrew as plainly as he could and waited for me to gather myself. As for me, shock had redefined itself. My eyes had suddenly refused to see anything, my mind had stopped working, and I was not able to hear anything at all. I did not know whether I was still standing or had I collapsed. Was I in my senses or had I fainted? But I was stunned for sure.

"I only came back to my senses when Lord Andrew drew me close to him, and shock melted as tears through my eyes. I felt my mind had frozen. It had ceased to reason, thus it took a continuous flow of tears that helped my mind to warm up and question. 'You did a background check on me?' I questioned Lord Andrew. 'With the utmost and uncompromising responsibility of guarding the repute that our family has earned over generations of sacrifice and heroism, it's imperative that we follow certain norms about anybody we wish to have ties with, my dear. But in your case I did not have to do so,' answered Lord Andrew, and continued, 'One of your professors now, and your father studied in Cambridge together. They had kept in touch and it was he who told me all about you. He did not wish to reveal his past to you for reasons better known to him and did not want me to do so either, but unfortunately your relation with my son left me no choice other than this. Therefore I wish to tell you once again that you should distance yourself from Edward, and as far as your education is concerned, you have proven to be a well deserving seeker of knowledge and it is my personal responsibility to see that nothing less than the best is made available to you.' Lord Andrew did not say a word more as he walked me to his car waiting to drive me home. Chivalry doesn't fail to make its presence at such moments too as he opened the door of the car, and shut it gently after I was seated comfortably. His eyes did not meet mine after that and we both moved in opposite directions.

"What a Sunday that had been for me! That morning I was nurturing dreams of settling down some day in a family that I could say was mine, and that same afternoon I was driving out and away from the same house with an understanding of a gruesome fact that even though bastards were not at fault of being so, yet they could not rid themselves of the condemnation their parents deserved to face. It just goes to reflect the ruthlessness of society, when they need to punish, they don't seem to distinguish between the innocent and the guilty. Why should bastards have to pay the price for their parents' casual pleasures otherwise? In my case, I had parents that willingly gave me their name, looked after me as one of their own yet no amount of merit I earned could help wash away one stigma that equalled or superseded all my achievements. At least I was responsible for my achievements, and as for paternity, who has had the liberty to choose one for themselves? Our pretentious modernity, once again proved crippled without the support of the crutches of our antiquated dogmas.

"It was not difficult for me to guess which professor could be the one who retained the keys to the secret diary of my life, but why did this have to happen at all, I wondered. Was happiness and contentment always going to behave miserly to me? I was angry and remorseful at the same time. As time and distance passed, calmness entered my mind; I thought to myself, was it better that Lord Andrew learnt of this before we went any further? For, had this revelation happened after I had been married to Edward, they all would have believed that I had deceived them by keeping dark facts of my past to myself.

"Reality is dual in nature. It hurts you very much when it peels off the outer layer and reveals the true scenario in its pure and naked form. The pain in the beginning seems worthy when it helps one realise that what had happened was meant to, eventually. I was fortunate that facts dawned upon me at the right time and saved me from committing grave errors ahead. On one hand I had lost Edward for ever, on the other even if I would have gained him for now, I would have lost him for life, later. Only when one distances oneself from reality in time does one realise that what had happened was not because it was destined, but because with the character of people who had to decide upon such an issue could not have come up with any other plausible solution.

"Officer, I hope this incident of my life would prove to you that I am quite capable of digesting setbacks with a pinch of salt. I have gotten used to the loss of everything I have loved."

"Rosha, at the present moment I am wondering why did you deserve to season yourself to obstacles when others deserved it more than you? But, before you explain the nitty-gritty's of it, I request you to get along with what you did next. We are approaching the airport and would be there sooner than we expect."

❑❑❑

19

A Chest of Secrets

"It was not difficult to gauge which of my professors could have been privy to my past and a friend of Edward's family too. Dr Robert R Whitmore was my tutor that Edward had chosen to groom me before I appeared for my entrance exams, as I did not have the formal eligibility required for admission. Dr Whitmore was the one who had introduced me to the concept of what thinking meant to thinkers and how much of their thoughts have been actively used by humanity for centuries. He was the one who had generously answered all my questions and spent hours after work preparing me for the test. He was in his late fifties then, as old as my father would have been, if alive.

"Dr Whitmore had only once asked me about my father's name and that was it. Rest, he said he knew all that he wanted to know about me. I assumed that Edward must have told him all that he needed to know about me. Besides that one query in regards to my father, there had never been any reason or pretext where family members could have found mention.

"On several occasions in the past I had accompanied him on long walks across the Hyde Park and had enlightening discussions with him while he walked his golden retriever. By the time I arrived at my apartment, showered, and stepped out once again, I knew at that time of the day where I could hope to find Dr Whitmore. I did not seem to care much about formalities, thus did not call him beforehand.

"When Dr Whitmore noticed me approaching him, he did not try acting innocent or unaware of the situation. He was a man, who did not like to waste time in mincing words, creating unbelievable excuses or emotional apologies. Thus as I walked closer to him, he looked in my eyes and knew that his fears had just come true. 'I am sorry child, I always felt that I should not have told them everything,' said Dr Whitmore in a sombre tone. 'But then Lord Andrew is no ordinary person and if he designated me with the responsibility to teach you, I had to keep him abreast with your progress and everything else I learnt about you. Besides if he were to find out that I knew your family, before I could tell him so… then I don't need to tell you what I would have been reduced to.' This way Dr Whitmore concluded his defence and I heard all of it without saying a word. Now, it was my turn to ask him a question – 'Did you really know my father so well?'

'Yes, I did and have known him until the day he was shot. We spoke on the phone that very evening and exchanged greetings for the year to come. Unfortunately, the new year was never to dawn in your father's life. We went to college together and graduated the same year – 1972. We kept writing to each other occasionally until we met again, here in London in autumn of 1976. I had just completed my PhD and returned from the United States of America. Your father was beginning to think of expanding his family business to the West and was visiting London for that purpose. He also shared the fact that his parents were eager to get him married and he was evading responsibility for the time being.

'It was only later when the Soviets started penetrating into Afghanistan that your father and I communicated more frequently to discuss various issues. Those years brought us very close. Overall, your father transformed into a hero battling the Soviets and collaborating with the CIA and American envoys for the want of weapons and medicine. After doing all that, he did not deserve to meet such a death. What a shame!'

'Dr Whitmore, I don't seem to see myself surface anywhere so far,' I said after being a patient listener. 'Why of course you would surface only after your mother does, isn't it? Your father got married in 1982 or 83 if I remember it correctly. It was not an ordinary marriage. It was probably one of its kinds to have happened. Your father had decided to marry a barren woman to prove a point that just because a woman could not bear a child did not mean that she did not deserve enough to be loved and cared for. The orthodox clerics were up in arms, his family threatened to disown him, but your father stood his ground. He challenged if anybody who could reason with him and convince him that he was setting a bad example, he was ready to face any sort of punishment to have rebelled against the rules of the faith. Nobody came forward to accept his challenge. He married your mother, a beautiful charming girl who had been abandoned by her earlier husband for not being able to breed. She was illiterate, but your father educated her and from there he got the inspiration to open a school for children who could not afford one and for those adults who did not realise the importance of one.

'Since he had established links in the Western world, money reached him whenever he needed it, I was more than willing to help in any way I could and managed to send him loads of books for the library and film reels that could be screened for the children. One late evening as he described it in one of his letters, he witnessed an unwed mother abandon her child in the early hours one morning. Your father brought that child home and named her Aashna meaning faith, am I right?'

'Yes doctor, it means faith, indeed. So was I also born out of some reckless encounter?' 'No one knows where you came from. As your father mentioned in one of his many letters to me, that someone must have left you close to the rose bushes in his garden. Just look at the way Nature helps one who is meant to survive! Those thorny bushes protected you from street dogs and other animals that could have relished your soft flesh overnight, had you been left in the open. Since that was where he found you shivering and squealing due to the chill and hunger, he named you Rosha. Why don't we go home, I will show you his letters and the manner in which he described each one of you. I had to handover all this to you some day; I think that day happens to be today.'

"Dr Whitmore was a loner and probably avoided handling people in their emotional moments. I had just learnt the reality of my first day of life – abandoned in the rosebush so that the thorns could prick me and I might bleed to death, or probably a young, helpless girl found no other place better than that one to leave me and rid her of the stigma. Who would ever know for a fact? However, I followed Dr Whitmore to his apartment, as he did not offer me any time to remorse or delve over the past. He wanted me to build stronger from within and face the future.

"At Dr Whitmore's house, I went through pictures, letters, souvenirs that my father had sent him for keepsake. They still had the smell of home in them. A beautifully carved rosewood chest housed a family in it that once lived and thrived happily I thought and remarked, I wonder what my father did to have called for his own death. I mean all that I have seen so far, only goes to show that he was more than loyal to his Nation, to its people and to his family.

'You know, Rosha, your father had grown habituated to taking the bull by its horns. Often your father won the challenge and kept going for it repeatedly, missing a point that he was enraging the bull beyond limits. Unfortunately, one day the bull got the better of him.

'Let me make it simpler and more direct. He was associated with the CIA and the US State department during the Soviet invasion. Back then, your country had very few men who could communicate in English and almost none who could communicate with the flair your father could. That time aid from the US was welcomed and your father had turned a *messiah* for his men.

'He arranged training camps for young men who could train in warfare and so on. Eventually they managed to oust the Soviets. Thus, he was forgiven for marrying a barren woman and for adopting two orphaned children. No one could dare speak against him. It is a different issue that he was not wrong in whatever he had done. However, the religious gentry were waiting for a chance to knock him down.

'Your father was aware of all that but he did not bother. Then one day he brought home a little male child – your younger brother. He was spotted roaming the streets of Kabul, when your father recognised him to be a son of a soldier who had recently died of some epidemic.'

'What he told us was that he was our cousin who had unfortunately lost his parents in an accident. Since he had no home to go to, father had decided that Zahid would stay with us. But, I clearly remember that we witnessed our mother's belly growing bigger as she did give birth to Jehan, my youngest brother. She had gone to the hospital for a good one month and when she returned with Jehan, he indeed was just little over fifteen days old?'

"Dr Whitmore looked at me as I shared my curiosity with him and then he sifted through some letters and handed me one of them to read. It was a letter from my father. He mentioned in that of how important it was for a woman to become a mother. He wrote – Even though the process demanded a lot of care, restraint, and pain, yet a woman would yearn to give birth. As for his wife, who could never give birth, the charade of a false pregnancy was essential as Aashna, Rosha and Zahid were grown up enough to understand how a baby formed in a mother's womb. It also gave his wife a satisfaction of at least pretending to bear a child.

"The curious women in the neighbourhood did not give up, and kept visiting to find out the secret behind such an immaculate conception. All this was necessary as the child to be born was going to be born to a woman who had been sentenced to death. Her death sentence would be carried out after she gave birth. It was absurd, when one thought about such a proposition. Who would take the responsibility of the child? The State would send it to an orphanage and they would in turn dispose it off in some foxhole for it was against the norms of Islam to house a child of woman condemned to death for adultery.

"A child was about to arrive into a world where people were anxiously waiting to rid him within a few hours of his birth. If it were to be a boy, my father had written that he would name him – Jehan, he believed that if it survived he would symbolise the existence of humanity in the world.

"Another letter that Dr Whitmore passed on to me just as I finished this one described the drama that surrounded Jehan's birth. It revealed how my father had pulled strings in the UN and with some of his old friends from the US embassy to put pressure on the jail authorities to declare that the child was still born.

"The curious fanatics headed by their clerics gathered at the gates of the prison for days to claim their victim but ultimately had to be satisfied with the doctor's verdict that the child was born dead. The religious masters were relieved and proclaimed that Almighty had done justice. As for my father, he retreated to a hill station near Kabul and let my mother nurse the child – Jehan, for a few weeks before they returned home. I can never forget how excited we three were, when we had welcomed our youngest brother and how we quarrelled to play with him and carry him in our arms.

"Tears welled up in my eyes as I returned the letter to Dr Whitmore and said – why should such a saviour be murdered by those very people whom he had protected?

"Dr Whitmore caressed me and said there is a need of selflessness because selfishness exists. Sometimes the selfless win and at times it's the turn of the selfish. These are two essential halves of humanity. It won't exist otherwise.

"He then handed me the rosewood chest asking me to keep it with me as it was family heirloom and I was the one who should keep it from then on. To me, that Sunday had been nothing less than a rollercoaster ride in time. I was least capable of carrying my own burden back home with me, and to add to it this heirloom, made it just impossible for me. I told Dr Whitmore that I would definitely accept it one day, but that day was not the right one for the purpose. He did not insist and I took his leave, thanking him for solving all the remaining unsolved mysteries that surrounded my past life.

"On my way back home, as all those thoughts reeled through my mind, I realised that I had been very foolish to think of getting married to Edward. For some time, I had conveniently forgotten what the doctor had told me in Saudi Arabia. Even if the coincidence of Dr Whitmore knowing my father and Lord Andrew were not to occur, I would remain a barren woman, anyways. How I missed that point, I wondered. How could I have not revealed this to Edward? Why had the rosy dreams of a beautiful future blinded me so severely that I had conveniently forgotten to reveal such an important fact to Edward? On the other hand, was I plain selfish? I knew one thing for sure that I had not kept it from him intentionally. That evening when I bathed, I washed myself off all regrets I had gathered that day and thanked God for saving me from committing a grave folly of getting married to Edward and turning him into the last surviving heir of an illustrious family that had lasted over so many centuries.

"Officer, from that day on, college, books, thinkers, prophets, and their philosophies became my world. I had gathered enough in terms of memories and experiences that could last me a lifetime, now I had to learn how to reason them correctly."

As she opened a bottle of water to take a few sips, our car turned around a curb and my eyes shifted from her to notice the luminous neon sign – 'Chhatrapati Shivaji International Airport'.

❑❑❑

20

Untying the Final Tangle

There was not much paperwork left for me to do at the airport as Rosha's deportation documents and those needed for the other thirteen deportees were already in our possession. While they were taken to the deportee hold area, I completed the check-in formalities for Rosha and a few others.

While waiting at that check-in counter, I wondered what she had done to deserve a life so severe. Right from the time she was abandoned in a thorny rose bush, thorns had in fact proved to be her protectors in a way. Nevertheless, one cannot ignore the pain they must have given her, whenever fate tossed her the wrong way. Yet, she had proven to be a blooming rose, standing tall above all the thorns.

However, curiosity still kept nudging me, as I did not know where and what had Rosha done to deserve to be sent back to the same hell she had once escaped. Why did she leave England at all? Was she made to do so? Such questions could have various combinations and permutations of various circumstances woven into each other, thus one could end up weaving an unwanted yarn out of it.

A colleague of mine joined me in my waiting and informed that a few deportees had already boarded their respective flights. Five were to board in an hour or so and Rosha was probably going to leave last. Moving away from the counter to share a cup of tea, he noticed that I wasn't my usual self. He was aware that I was listening to Rosha's story all the way to the airport, but he did not wish to admit that he had relished the juicy gossip that my other colleagues in the car must have narrated about Rosha and me.

His consolidated curiosities came out in a simple question – "Doesn't seem like you have slept at all?" I knew exactly where he was coming from and thus did not waste time in replying honestly.

I said, "Yes indeed, how could anyone who was to hear what that poor girl had to go through?"

My colleague gauged from my answer and the tone of my voice that Rosha had struck a deep chord in me.

He said, "Anyone would sympathise with such a beautiful girl, besides I believe she was pursuing PhD here."

Now, this was least of the turn I was expecting Rosha's story to take. I wondered if my curiosity to know all about her life would be satiated before she left. With some lousy pretext, I excused myself from the company of my colleague and headed straight to the deportee hold area with Rosha's documents and boarding card in my hand.

As I approached the door of that room, I saw Rosha through the glass wall. It seemed as though an angel was sleeping. I was sure that she must have been tired and needed to catch some sleep before she left. But I wanted to know about the rest of her journeys, upheavals, and achievements.

As I took a step forward and ordered a constable to wake her up, I wondered, now that her deportation had turned from irreversible to a reality, would she even want to reveal any further to me? I did not care. I had to take my chances and as she woke up and saw me, she smiled gently and walked towards me. I said to her, "Madam, your formalities are completed; you need to follow me to clear immigration." Rosha obeyed and off I was with a hope to find out the rest about her.

While I walked her to the immigration, I did not speak a word to her, thus keeping the scene as formal as I could. As I handed over her documents to the immigration officer, he glanced at me for a moment and knew who I was and then he froze as he got his eyes on Rosha. For a few moments, even he seemed smitten by her beauty, until I had to remind him that he had a job to do besides daydreaming.

Rosha's flight was a good two hours fifteen minutes from the time she cleared immigration and entered the security area meant for travelling passengers only. Once seated in a sprawling and comfortable seat, I asked her if I could get her something to eat or drink. She refused.

I asked her, "Do you really don't want anything to eat or drink or is it because you are disheartened?"

"A bit of both I guess, officer. Everybody is aware that death is imminent but when it occurs, it makes you sad… and so am I at this moment. Some inexplicable miracle could have saved me from this I thought, but maybe I don't deserve it."

"Why do you say that, Rosha? If there is anybody who deserved a miracle it had to be you."

"I am being honest when I say this to you; I have not seen anyone like you who had the courage to battle one's own demons and conquer all that would seem unthinkable to anyone who would have found herself in your situation. Assuming if there were ten women to have found themselves in your position, I think five would have ended their own lives, two would have accepted all that came their way, by considering it to be fate, two would have tried once or twice or given up in time, and someone like yourself, who had the might of wisdom at your side, would have succeeded."

"What is the use of such success that benefits no one else? It will all go with me, while you were away I was telling myself that had I stay put in London and got a job somewhere, life would have been better, but knowledge does strange things to people. While you seek it ardently, it unfurls itself gradually, layer after layer and when you think you have gained so much of it that you are strong enough to use it like a pen or a sword that same knowledge transforms into might. Now I realise that this is the critical moment that one should be very careful about – when wisdom bestows its seeker with its might, it can drive a knowledgeable king like Ravana to his death over an unbelievably lousy pretext or have Jesus urge to the Lord to forgive his own murderers. Whichever way you look at it, the tool of knowledge drives one to scale that height which one thinks would be impossible to achieve, but once there, one thinks he is limitless and that's where the beginning of his failure sets in.

"I guess when I decided to leave England for research, my failure stepped in, and today it is standing right in front of me, reminding me of all those who earnestly requested me to stay back, while I was persistent on pursuing my goals further."

What could I say to a girl whose speed of thought from past to present, from philosophy to existing day situations, equalled that of a shooting star? Unfortunately, even this shooting star was aware that it was going to fade away soon. There was no point in consoling her, as she was not the type who needed it and I was not the one to say anything without being sure of it myself.

Therefore, I found it best to take her back in time, into her apartment after she had visited Dr Whitmore.

I said, "Rosha, can we continue from where we had left?"

She looked at me, tad longer than a usual moment. Her look had almost intimidated me to give her an explanation about why I wanted to know further.

Fortunately, it did not come to that as she answered in one word "Of course!" and off we were once again to untie the remaining threads from the tangle.

❑❑❑

21

Parting to Meet Again

"After that fateful Sunday, the only other thing that kept putting me off gear, from time to time, was Edward's complete absence from my life. London was not the same city without him. I had very few or no memories at all of London alone, besides the time I would spend in college and while browsing through old books that had long been out of print and were only to be found at Oxford street in the array of second-hand bookstores that would keep them. Until I began stepping out on my own for everything else too, I missed Edward extremely. For months, I was reminded of Edward for as little as the bus I took to college turned around Leicester Square or crossed the Ritz hotel. We had indeed shared beautiful evenings on those streets, just walking through them, and imagining ourselves to keep doing so until death would do us apart.

"Even though I had kept my word to Lord Andrew by not even trying once to contact Edward, I wondered what could have stopped him from doing so. It did take a long while before I could get used to the thought of not expecting to see Edward anymore or ever again. As for the apartment he had arranged for me, it continued to be mine and college expenses were taken care of too, as promised by Lord Andrew. I received details of a bank account from which I could withdraw up to two thousand pounds a month for my expense. Lord Andrew was my guardian in college records and monetary terms, but it was Dr Whitmore who became my primary channel of communication between Edward's family and me. He had agreed to do so on one condition laid out right on the onset of this proposition. He had told me that I would never use his good faith to enquire about Edward. I had kept my word and he had never failed in his commitment in return.

"All said and done, I just could not understand what could have stopped Edward from meeting me just once, only to say goodbye for that matter. I mean he was a man who had done the most rebellious act by asking me to leave Saudi Arabia and had arranged for the same. He had the courage to take me around and introduce me to his world as a person worthy of such respect, and then all of a sudden, if such a mentor and lover were to disappear from my life as instantly as he had appeared, it was very hard to hold myself from not enquiring about him at all. Unlike my family, Edward was not dead.

Thus, it was not easy to come to terms with reality and prevent myself from seeking a way out. But with no options in sight and with the passing time, I assumed that Edward's parents might have reasoned with him about the prospective future of their clan with a barren woman as the bride.

"The more I focused my attention on learning, the more it revealed to me about the way life has been for many and most of us. I realised that we have tried ourselves with similar emotions for centuries, have had similar questions ages ago too, had probably found the right solutions also, but had failed to accept and implement those. Even I knew that there was no point thinking of Edward. It was in best of our interests that we never met again, but then how could I just wipe away the memory of the man I was so deeply in love with? As much as I tried to engage myself with studies, my writings, or friends, I would still manage to find an idle moment that would remind me of Edward and would also leave me disheartened in the end.

"A good six months of efforts got me used to the fact that it was all over between us and I had to be thankful to his family for the favour they had bestowed upon me in exchange. I had to move on as Edward might have already. Dr Whitmore and other professors were reasonably impressed and supported me wholeheartedly by guiding me in my writings, essays based on the thoughts and theories put forward by earlier thinkers, because I belonged to a Continent where thinkers had never separated their thoughts from spirituality. Whereas in the West both were considered two different things altogether.

"The unique blend of my erstwhile upbringing, the chequered graph of my life so far and the present guidance offered me an advantage of grasping the subjects faster than the others could. Ethics, morality, need for religion, and politics etc were complicated to understand. Those pioneers of thought, I understood, were being questioned, and that too in a time when our race was still required to wait a good three to four hundred years before which, they could witness the advent of a few who we know and revere as prophets or founders of faith today. However, the trial and tribulations those early thinkers had to go through in order to get there were not difficult to relate to. Experiences with people and the world around me, now and before, acted as a link that would help me walk into the world millenniums away in terms of time and see people not very different at the core from what I would find on my way back into our present day world.

"People were then ready to damn those deserving thinkers if they stood between them and profit; it still is the same. What is different though is that those great thinkers did spend years over debating and experimenting on such matters, and left behind for us a rich treasure of probable solutions, which could have solved our troubles to a great extent, provided we implement those, rather than just research those theories, applaud them, appreciate them if we wished to, but never practise them. On a lighter note, who would want to do so, because most of those who founded such theories had to pay with their own lives for it. Even today, one would have to pay the same price, I guess.

"Man has been most curious of that unknown to him and the most scared too. If these thinkers were able to achieve what they did, was because they were encouraged by their rulers, or patronised by the wealthy and prominent people of those times. Nevertheless, when the thinker, after putting in years of toil came up with his find, these very supporters would take very little time to scheme the death of a hero. What happened to Galileo, for instance? He enjoyed the support of Vatican until he revealed that the earth was round and not flat, thus challenging the merits of the Holy Bible.

"Those very men, who had provided him with the means for research, reduced Galileo's works to ashes. However, his find did create a second thought in people's minds. Therefore, even though the merit of the Holy Bible remained unquestioned, Galileo's found place in the academia of those times as an alternate theory. There were several such paradoxes that I came to learn about. However, the glory of their perseverance and the single-mindedness with which they strived forward left very little or no reason to ponder on what happened with what they had discovered or granted to the world. They had proven themselves to be valiant conquerors by conquering what they had set their sight on. They had made a place for themselves in history. Whether one adopted what they prescribed or otherwise, they had to be acknowledged.

"On the other hand, what more could man do, for he did not have the courage to follow and practise what was suggested and could not end up being regarded foolish to have not done so either. Therefore, he learnt the easy way out – acknowledge the genius of the inventor and leave the rest to time, politics, and society to agree to the same. When majority of humankind agree to accept it, then he would join in too and try to impose his distinction of having known so and so and his such and such find much before anybody had even heard his name."

"He would then find a means to capitalise on something that he had trashed and long forgotten. Somewhere the seers knew the reactions they would have to make do with, thus nothing mattered to them. Neither appreciation nor condemnation affected them. They taught the princely as well as the not-so-privileged-ones without any prejudice. They had realised long ago what to expect from people and thus they had no complaints with whatever came their way.

"We admit that we cannot become like them because we are not left with much to do with life besides loving a few and then complaining about those same we loved, then turn love into hatred and anger, later turn anger into contempt and ultimately end up being unhappy ourselves. We just cannot come to terms with the fact that nothing has existed for eternity and nothing would. I am not saying this for the sake of it, but believe me a year later when I passed my class with distinction and my essays got a few modern thinkers interested in my work too, I was invited to a party where I would find an opportunity to meet a few of those, whose works I had studied already.

"It was quite an experience to interact with those knowledgeable men. As Dr Whitmore introduced me to most of them, others found it their duty to introduce themselves and were charmed and intrigued to know that I was the one who had travelled half the globe to pursue such stream of education when most of my kind would be seen queuing up at business schools. Dr Whitmore and me lost each other in the company of the luminaries and I wandered to gather some fresh air in the sprawling lawns when my eyes fell on a beautiful, well dressed young girl, probably a few years elder than I was then.

"She heard my footsteps when the tiny pebbles of gravel grinded against my shoes, as I walked across onto the lawn. Dressed in a rich beige evening gown, her face seemed radiant in that sparse lit exteriors. We exchanged pleasantries and introduced ourselves. Her name was Claire; she was the daughter of one of the very affluent and leading business magnates of Europe. I wondered what was somebody of her kind doing in such a place. Claire revealed that her father believed that thinkers had the capability to see future and he liked their company because he knew how to transform vision into business. I smiled for more than one reason and probably Claire understood it too as she responded similarly.

"We spoke of everything we could. She was learning business under her father's tutelage after graduating from a renowned business school there and she had walked out a few moments before me to catch a breath of fresh air, just like me. 'So are we too going to form a friendship like your father does where I would have the vision of the future and you would have the acumen to transform it into a business?' I said to Claire. That jovial question really broke the ice between us and then onwards we chatted as any two girls would.

"Unfortunately, that bond was going to shatter much before it could form. A heavy male voice called Claire back inside, while I chose to stay outside for a while. Moments later Claire walked towards me accompanied with Edward. I lost my balance for a moment as I rose to stand. Claire introduced me to her fiancé, and I met him with all the expressions that one should have on one's face while meeting somebody for the first time. Claire hailed from Manchester, therefore she might not have known about Edward and me I thought. On the contrary, she knew all about us and I was to find this out a day later when Edward visited me.

"That night I remained disturbed briefly, but I could not fall asleep. I thought to myself that while I had lost sense of day and time, immersed in the ocean of knowledge, I had travelled so far, so soon that Edward had managed to forget and let go of the moments we had shared and the time we had spent together. I did not regret any of it, neither was I angry over anything or anybody, but I kept thinking that I had not even looked at any other boy in all this while and Edward was already engaged.

"Next evening when I answered the door and saw him alone in front of me, it took a lot of courage in me to prevent myself from giving into his advances. I had just showered and stepped out with my hair still wet, the exact look that would turn on Edward and I looked no different that evening. It was good on his part to restrict himself well in time too. For one moment I feared that I was about to be raped by the man I had dearly loved once. On the other hand, what difference should it have made to a woman who was used to being a keep, I thought. I was no more anybody's keep and I did not wish to remain the beloved of someone who was committed already.

'What made you gatecrash Edward?' I questioned him. He wished to curse fate for what it had brought us to, while I kept telling him that we chose what we wanted to and no hard feelings should exist anymore. I also gave in the secret of me never being able to produce a child and told him that that could have been more unfortunate than us not getting married. This fact calmed him largely and rid him of his guilt. That night we went out to dine as friends and said our goodbyes.

"Six months later, I received an invitation to Edward and Claire's wedding, which I attended and wholeheartedly wished them the very best. The Lord and the Lady seemed more than thankful to me to have stepped aside so gracefully from Edward's life and saved them from heaps of embarrassment. While I accepted their gratitude, I could only tell them how grateful I was to have their continued generosity towards me.

"That day as I stepped out of the chapel, I had once again stepped out of a period in life that was not meant to be revisited ever again. My pursuit for knowledge grew even stronger as I had no commitments towards anyone in person anymore. Therefore, while I turned a graduate with honours in years to come, Edward and Claire turned proud parents of their first child – a son. By the time, I was preparing for my Masters submissions, Claire had already filed for divorce as she found it very difficult to cope with Edward's family. She had decided to move to Los Angeles with legal custody of their child. Her divorce plea also had a mention of me as one of the other reasons.

"Lawyers can really help one recollect their past better than anyone else does and then reinterpret those memories in such a way that they benefit their client today, even if they did not matter much to you in the past. I pitied the Lord and the Lady more than anybody else did. What would have been more embarrassing I thought – Edward marrying an orphaned barren bastard from Afghanistan and leading a happy life or exchanging vows with the daughter of a flourishing business tycoon, who just could not model herself in accordance to aristocracy?

"I knew, all this and separation from the child would turn Edward vulnerable and there was a bright chance that he would come knocking at my door and turn me into his succour. If such a disaster were to happen, it would result in millions of pounds to be paid to Claire in compensation due to promiscuity of her husband being proven. I would lose all the respect I had gathered over the years in the hearts of Edward's parents, Dr Whitmore and many more who found it honourable to help me in whichever way they could but never be able to accept me as one of them.

"Dr Whitmore was surprised when I requested him to arrange a meeting with Lord Andrew, nonetheless he obliged. I met Lord Andrew at his farm and he seemed equally shocked on hearing what I had requested to meet him for. I had decided to leave England for good and pursue my PhD in some other country. This would keep me out of reach from Edward and would save his family of any further embarrassment. 'After all that you have achieved, you are thinking of quitting,' questioned Lord Andrew. 'On the contrary, your Lordship,

I am thankful to you to have nursed a fledgling that is now ready to fly and take on the journey it needs to,' I replied. Lord Andrew looked into my eyes for a few moments. He too had developed a kind of liking for me over the years and that moment was to become his test of emotional strength. 'I think you first decide how you wish to pursue your life further, and send me your plans in writing through Dr Whitmore. I shall decide on its viability and inform you of my opinion on the same. I hope, being your legal guardian for the past so many years, offers me this right at least.'

"Even though Lord Andrew tried hard to be formal and authoritative, I could sense the plea in what sounded like a command. I could not hold myself for too long as we hugged each other and I cried like any daughter would when she would leave her father's home one last time to begin a new life with new people and in a new family. As for Lord Andrew, he had secretly developed hopes to see me rise and shine one day. Unfortunately, I was suggesting an end to his dreams he thought. I promised him that I would not take a step out of his permission and in exchange urged him never to assume that I would forget their kindness and generosity so easily.

"It was indeed a very emotional moment that had come in my life after a very long time. I was glad that I had managed to earn the love and respect of someone that once could not think of me more than a muse of their son. Once again, that day, Lord Andrew walked me to his car and saw me off. As I drove back this time though, I had to think of what I wanted to do and where did I wish to go. Just as years ago I had to seek advice from Dr Whitmore, it was the case that day too.

It seemed a strange coincidence though that whenever Lord Andrew saw me off, I would have to meet Dr Whitmore after that. So once again, that evening we met at Hyde Park and then walked back to his apartment. Last time it was to know about my past, and this time, to help me chart out my future."

❑❑❑

22

Nomadic Intentions

What could I say to interrupt Rosha? What did I have to ask her either. She was coming out with everything she had. All I could do was keep looking at her and listen. But it wasn't easy. One could not plainly listen and let go of what she had to say. It made one think too at the same time. It just kept me wondering how unpredictable life can be to some. Not that it isn't the case with everybody, but with a select few, life is comparatively more generous in revealing its true self – Unpredictability.

As she excused herself to the restroom, I thought why I was supposed to learn about her; besides would she have told it to anybody that could have been with her that night? Was it a test in some way to do justice to her as human, rather being an imposing law keeper? I kept questions to myself as she walked back. Her story had yet not come up to the time where I had knocked on the door of her flat. She settled down next to me, moistened her throat with a few sips of water and took me along with her to Dr Whitmore's apartment in London.

"When I had first met Dr Whitmore at the Hyde Park, he knew why I was there. But, the second time round he seemed puzzled, and when we stepped into his house he told me, 'Last time you had the questions and I had answers to them, but now I have a question and probably you would have an answer to it. Why do you wish to punish yourself for nothing?' questioned Dr Whitmore. 'I don't think I am punishing myself in any way, Dr Whitmore. I just think that it would be better for me to study somewhere away from this country and explore the diversity of thought and thinkers that prevailed elsewhere.' 'If you think you are going to hide yourself from Edward by leaving, you are completely mistaken, I say. First of all I do not think he is going to turn you into his weeping shoulder, and even if he wanted to do so, do you think he won't be able to find out where you are?'

'Dr Whitmore, I think it might not be as easy as it sounds.' 'You are being biased about the decision you have made therefore I do not see any reason I should continue to argue with you about the real reason for which you wish to leave. So tell me what are you expecting from me?' 'I am sorry Dr Whitmore, but I did not mean to hurt you in any way. I want you to guide me to pick a worthy topic for my PhD – a topic that would take me to a different land altogether, far away from here for some years.'

"Dr Whitmore's eyes and face looked tired for having tried as much as he could to stop me from leaving London. One reason for him to have given up was that he knew that I had already convinced myself beyond doubt that I was leaving and it was the only solution to prevent any further chaos amongst the members of Edward's family. I was not guilty or the conspirer of Claire's break-up with Edward, therefore I did not want to be victimised for no reason. There was no other solution besides bidding adieu to London. Where to was the question and Dr Whitmore's answer to that was, 'Since you were born in Afghanistan and have lived your childhood years over there, I suggest you should aim for a research of seers who belonged to the Sufi line of thought. Many mystics were born in Afghanistan and then travelled the world over, interacting with thinkers of their times and spreading their finds in exchange. I suggest you look for some unsung hero amongst them and show me the ones you choose.'

"It was indeed a right suggestion that Dr Whitmore had voiced. By doing so, I would be learning more about a world that I had once belonged to and probably understand the root cause of the problems it was facing today. That evening I had found a direction, courtesy Dr Whitmore. I still had the daunting task of finding out which Sufi saint was going to be my subject for research. I had no idea of what was I looking for in a world of *dervishes, fakirs,* or mystics that would compel me to research his life.

"Days went by as I kept skimming through pages and pages of history of Sufism, its basic pillars of thought, the reasons it formed for and the generations of *dervishes,* that had come to be. Unlike most of the thinkers that I had read about, Sufis were a tad different. As compared to the Western thinkers, these mystics were seekers who had surrendered themselves to the existence of a Supreme Lord and they would seek his company everywhere, every time, in everything they did. They were a kind of people to whom their own lives did not matter much unless their beloved was not by their side.

"These people romanced God. Their love and surrender to the Almighty reflected endlessly in their poetries, songs, and writings. They were not the god fearing types, but on the contrary addressed him as their beloved. Most of the seers and *fakirs* following the Sufi tradition led nomadic lives, until they would feel that they should stop. Then that is where they would camp until they felt they needed to move again or else they would remain in the same place, be it a roadside, a village or a huge city, for the rest of their lives and share their wisdom with the locals, in the form of songs and poetry.

"The illiterate masses could understand the preaching of such masters as they would simplify complex matters and put them across to the people in a manner they could understand. Innumerable poetry and songs thus composed have been hummed by millions for centuries to come and today millions of such verse passed on verbally from generation to generation has found itself rested in books, which an altogether different world is able to read and realise for themselves that the quest to know more was the same among the people world over. East or West, humanity battled to find answers to the same questions, with similar solutions to find and almost identical issues to resolve. Even though, we realise the fact that humanity was no different in other parts of the world, one could not be compartmentalised into sections of race, cast, etc, yet in the end man preferred to live divided in terms of territory, wealth, and intellect.

"The unnecessary prejudice that a normal person would derive from his material possessions meant nothing to those Sufi *fakirs*. They were richer in their thought. Many kings would bow down at the feet of such *fakirs* requesting them to communicate their unfulfilled desires to the Supreme Lord. There were countless number of miracles that such *fakirs* had been commended for, by the nobles and the commons alike. Those seekers were such that their generosity had unimaginable limits and their wrath was equally destructible in nature. Therefore, people adhered to their prescribed norms faithfully and such *dervishes* came to be respected as saints, who have people visit their shrines to this day and the lucky few witness miracles of the mystical powers in today's modern age too. While I was going through many such instances, it occurred to me that all of them were men. It was a thought that made me put all my work aside and ponder over it for a while.

"It intrigued me no end to come to terms with the fact that none of the women of those times was interested in seeking what lay beyond what they were given. Or were they forbidden such liberties? It was hard to believe that no woman must have tried to follow the path of such *dervishes*. I had asked myself a simple question but the answer to the same was hard to find. Even though I had gone through facts and loads of works by the Sufi mystics, I was now bent on looking for one answer

– Did a female Sufi mystic exist ever? I shared that question with my teachers and friends who were not authorities on Sufism, but knew something about it. They seemed equally intrigued by it and equally ashamed for such a thought had never once occurred to them.

"Dr Whitmore was glad that I had come up with a curious angle for study. I later understood the true reason for his enthusiastic support. Dr Whitmore had realised that I had raised a question that would take a long time and hard work from my end to find an answer. Should it take longer than I expected, I would have no other choice but to renew my student's visa and pursue PhD in London itself. He knew that accomplishment of the task I had set my mind to was not that simple. Therefore, he encouraged me to dig further, and deeper as it would keep me engrossed and in London.

"After a very long gap of almost four years, wakefulness of time slipping away bothered me. It had been two weeks of searching through various books, journals, etc to find even a clue that could further my search. In all that, Edward's call took my anxiety levels to an altogether different high. My fears had indeed come true, when Edward expressed his desire to meet me. I did not refuse him altogether, but asked him to meet in a public place rather than at the apartment. He agreed and we met for dinner that same evening.

"On the contrary to what I thought, Edward did not utter any sentence urging for emotional support or any such thing. He just wanted to vent his frustration and anger over the fact that his father-in-law and his wife had played with his trust. His father-in-law indeed had businesses in Europe and interest of expanding across the Atlantic into the United States and Edward's family was foreseeing this collaboration as a speedy vehicle that would help them accomplish their own ambitions faster.

"While Edward's family had set their eyes on an even more extravagant future, they overlooked to notice the trap-laden path that lead to it. Over-confidence and good faith made Edward invest huge sums in businesses that were owned by the family he had married into. The companies he had invested in plummeted and by the time he realised that he had been cheated into a sham, it was too late as Claire was about to deliver their child.

"It was only after Edward hired a private investigator to look deeper into the whole matter that he learnt the real motives of his wife's side of the family. Their sudden shift from Spain to London, their instant and glitzy presence at important parties and social events was all a planned effort of Claire's father to fish a suitable and wealthy suitor/investor to pull him out of the red. Unfortunately, Edward bit into the hook called Claire.

"It was not as if Edward was nearing bankruptcy, but somebody within the family had taken their trust for granted and it was not something that could be ignored, forgotten, or forgiven easily. To render him further helpless, Claire was in custody of Edward's only child – the future scion of their family.

"It reminded me of the walk Lord Andrew and I had taken after the lunch meeting. I pitied him to have to deal with shattered dreams and an awkward embarrassment at his age. But, what else could they expect, I thought to myself. They had enough of everything and yet their urge for more did not seem to end. I still don't know why I spurted out those words, 'I think in all, it seems a very interesting setting of circumstances, Edward.'

"Edward was least expecting a statement of that nature from me. 'That is quite an unusual consolation,' he replied. Almost immediately I corrected myself by saying, 'I did not mean to hurt you any further, Edward, but I am not looking at all this in the same light as you are. I am thinking of it from a more general view, which drives me to conclude that money has proven to become the all pervading religion that has come to rule man, his faith, his beliefs, humanity and all that he stands for today. Money is a religion that does not distinguish between class, creed, sex, or morality. It favours all those who worship it and yearn to have the largest share of it, any which way possible. It also slaughters those who assume that they have found a way to rule over it. Its generosity equals its punishment. The greater your greed, worse the redemption. Therefore I do not know whether sympathy is what you exactly need. After all you chose to follow money as your principal faith and now you seem to regret its backlash. If you have realised the true nature of your Almighty then you would be peaceful once again and beware of its lure in the future.'

"Edward remained silent for a few moments and said, 'You think my marriage to Claire was some kind of business collaboration?' 'I guess you could answer the question better,' I replied. He seemed slightly clueless of what I was hinting at, thus I helped him find an answer by rephrasing my question, 'What do you think is troubling you more out of the two, the separation of your wife and child; or the millions you have already lost and more that you are going to lose in the coming days?' 'Rosha they conned me, my family, don't you see?' questioned Edward, evading to face reality. 'That answers your question, you fell for the lure of doubling your profits with a combination of beauty and wealth together,' I remarked. 'Edward, it just surprises me that you have forgotten those days when you loved me… it was pure… no strings attached, no money to be discussed and all we gave each other was pure love in return. In your relationship with Claire, there were other factors as important as her and if they all did not comply as per your expectations, you were bound to complain or regret your decision sooner or later,' I said to him. 'You were going to do nothing less than that I guess Rosha; you too had kept away a secret locked somewhere within you, so what difference does it make if I got fooled this way or that way, my goodness was taken for granted any which way you look at it,' replied Edward.

"That allegation of his was like a cold-blooded murderer claiming his victim. It had occurred to me once after separation that this fact could well result in undoing of our bond some day and it had turned into reality. I told Edward, 'I had not kept it from you intentionally, instead had forgotten all about it due to excitement you had caused in my life.' Edward kept looking at me. 'Edward, that look of yours is making me conscious,' I said to him. 'I wanted to meet you hoping to have your support instead you are showing me the mirror… anyways all the best with your future Rosha," said Edward, next moment he stood up and walked out of the restaurant. That was the last I saw of him. I do not know whether my thoughts hurt him more or he felt humiliated on hearing such words from his ex-lover. However, I did not feel sorry for whatever I had said. It might not have been the appropriate time, but when had time supported me with appropriation, I asked myself, as I paid the bill and stepped out of there.

"That evening I kept walking at a leisurely pace, observing, and absorbing everything that caught my attention. Somewhere deep within me I was feeling that the time to leave London was drawing close. Thus, I kept gathering all that I could put my eyes on as enduring visuals of London that would remain with me for time to come.

"I did not realise how far I had walked until I crossed over into Oxford Street. My feet had brought me to a place that brought a smile to my face. How could I have forgotten to visit Oxford Street of all the places? I had spent so much time there, browsing through books that were no longer to be found in stores. Some had outlived their potential and many that had no relevance in the present world. I had spent hours walking through that accumulated rubble of wisdom that seemed like relics of time that did not attract the attention of many today. But those few who ardently wandered around there were sure to set their eyes on a rare gem eventually. I had profited often in the past. That day, an overwhelming feeling of gratitude filled my heart as I glanced over the books while

I walked past those small stores one after the other. Little did I know that I would once again stumble upon a hidden treasure that very evening, once again and for the last time.

"An old leather bound book struggled to get out of the garbage bag as it tore through the plastic and fell on the street. A young boy who was carrying that garbage bag to the bin noticed it, he cursed the book for the damage it had done and continued towards the garbage bin to deposit the rest. That book lay there unclaimed as I walked towards it and picked it up. Before I could even dust it properly, that young lad stood there staring at me. I asked him the price and he replied in disgust, 'Keep it with best compliments from the dumps of Oxford Street.'

"I turned to look at the antiquated book. As I opened it, I realised that pages were missing from it and many were ready to free themselves from its bind. A little while later, I glanced at the title on the top of the page and I froze – 'A Sufi Matriarch', those words just stunned me beyond belief. I mean, I had spent weeks trying to get my hands on anything that could provide even a clue for that matter to prove that there once lived a woman Sufi *fakir,* and here I was holding a book on one. Indeed, I had stumbled upon a rare gem once again that day. A gem I had sought for weeks desperately. I had found the objective to my future all I had to do now was to chart a map for myself that would help me achieve my goals honourably."

❑❑❑

23

So Long London

"While I was reading about the Sufi seers, I also got to learn a lot about the Hindu and the Buddhist culture that was well prevalent in those times, besides Islam, Judaism, and Christianity. The *gurus* or seers of these Eastern faiths had one thing that distinguished them totally from the Western thinkers. They did not dispute the existence of God; instead, they sought a path to be able to commune with him. The masters of such devotion were revered and respected for their capabilities. They were also aware that they had a worldly duty to perform in the form of passing on his learning to the next generation and thus educate the young. Such gurus would put their students through various tests to analyse their endurance. Only when they were sure of one's capacity, would such masters take their pupils into the world they had discovered and belonged to.

"Something similar was happening with me too I thought on my way back to my apartment. From the time, I had set my mind to find out if there ever was a female seer, it had taken me two weeks of arduous search, and that day when I eventually found an answer to my question, it was in the form of a scrambled maze of loose pages of an old book. I would have to put bits and pieces together to prove my endurance to the saint. If she approved of my capability, only then I would be allowed to look further.

"It took me quite some time to establish a chronicle through the life and times of Hazrat Babajan that was what she was known as to the world, though her real name was Gulrukh, meaning 'Like a rose'. She was born in Baluchistan in 1806 and lived a good one hundred and twenty five years which took her to countries like Afghanistan, Pakistan, Syria, Iran, Iraq, Lebanon, Mecca and India.

"As I read the pages of her autobiography, I realised that it was a strange coincidence at play. She had lived a life very much similar to what I was leading myself and to further the similarities, her name did not mean much different from mine too. Even she had decided to walk out of her marriage and travel to find out about what exactly does the term God mean. She trained herself under various *gurus* and moved around countries with saints and seers who belonged to various or no specific faiths.

"Her travels finally brought her to India, where she spent time in Bombay, Nasik and eventually settled down in Poona. She lived under the serene shade of *Neem* (Margosa) tree for almost twenty-five years. Today her grave rests under that same tree and generations of her followers visit her grave to pay obeisance to the saint, every day.

"With a lot about her still missing in those lost pages, it was difficult to understand her real reasons for leading a life of a vagabond, not being stopped from doing so, not being tortured for doing so and all the reasons that could have stopped her from following her heart. However, the way she was addressed – Hazrat is an addressable to a male only. Therefore, even if she was a female saint and maybe the only one, which I was not sure about, people addressed her as Hazrat, a man.

"I had found my subject for study. I had found the country and the city I would make my home next, at least for a couple of years. As demanded by Lord Andrew, I sent him an elaborate write-up on the subject. My find had astonished both, Dr Whitmore and Lord Andrew alike. Dr Whitmore could not fathom, when, where and how I had stumbled upon such a discovery. On the other hand, Lord Andrew realised that it was impossible and rather unkind to stop me from pursuing what I had put my mind to. All the necessary arrangements were completed in time and I had decided to move around India as a bag packer. Similar to the nomadic way of life most of the Sufis or *sadhus* in India were known to follow.

"I planned to stay in small hotels initially and then organise to stay in a hostel or as a paying guest. I was not going to burden my guardian with extra expenses. Fortunately, a pound was well worth eighty-two Indian rupees then. Therefore, the two thousand pounds per month that I received in London seemed more than enough for my survival for a few months. The university had approved my subject for thesis and initial formalities would take a few weeks to complete once I reached there. All had happened well in time before my student's visa of UK was to expire.

"Finally, that day arrived when I had to bid adieu to London. As I drove to Heathrow, I remembered that sunny morning when I had stepped in and four years of eventful life was nearing its end with each mile the taxi headed further. I had thanked everybody wholeheartedly for having helped me generously to build myself.

"I had a tearful farewell with Lady Elizabeth. We met at their apartment, close to St James Court. It was a cosy place as compared to the palatial mansion they lived in. Lady Elizabeth and I met like mother and child. Probably it is instinctual that people who care for you genuinely, always tend to advise you and help you realise that they are genuinely concerned for your wellbeing. The way she went on with her dos and don'ts, neither could I stop her from instructing me nor could I stop my tears, until her own rolled down her cheeks. We hugged, we wept, we apologised to each other for everything. In me Lady Elizabeth must have found the daughter she never had and I had found the doting mother I had lost years ago.

"Dr Whitmore hid his tears behind his smile as he said, 'You are not going for ever, it's a matter of a couple of years at the most and I shall have arranged to lock you down here permanently on your return.' Lord Andrew could not make himself available as he was busy restructuring his business, helping his son resurrect from the losses they had earned. Edward was in Los Angeles accompanied with his lawyers to work out the alimony or arrive at a compromise with Claire.

"As I stepped out at Heathrow, I was shocked to see Lord Andrew waiting there, right in front of me, as though he were sure that the cab would stop at that very point. I ran towards him, as I would have towards my father. We hugged, we wept, I thanked him for all he had done and apologised for all the pain and heartache I must have caused him over the years. 'As a matter of fact, you helped us realise our faults, young girl,' said Lord Andrew. His eyes were still moist as he continued, 'Go on now, my child, and I wish you all the success in this world, I also expect you to keep in touch with me on phone and please drop in a word from time to time. I hope you know that I am still in love with the mail that arrives in an envelope, with stamps on it and the fragrance of the land it has travelled from. I have not come to terms with your new age emails as yet,' said Lord Andrew. I knew he loved my handwriting and the style in which I wrote.

"All said and done, it was time to leave. As the plane taxied to the runway, I watched the skyline of London and thought to myself that I did not have to be remorseful of my departure, as I did not intend to go away for ever. It was like a mission I set myself to and on its accomplishment, I would be back. This thought comforted me and seeped deep into my heart and mind. In a few minutes from that moment, the engines of the jumbo jet thundered to their fullest as though symbolising the commencement of my mission. With the sun setting in skies of London, I took off to a new land, new life, and a new mission."

❑❑❑

24

Welcome to India

"India was not one bit the same as it seemed in books, pictures, and television. In fact when I stepped foot in Delhi for the first time, I realised that people, animals, traffic and multitudes of colours all happened to hit you together, at the same time. She welcomed me with everything she had all at once. India was not anything like the countries I had lived in earlier. A lazing cow could sit in the middle of the street and continue ruminating leisurely while people would go about their own work without objecting to the obstruction it caused.

"Swanky cars would zoom past a majestic elephant walking on the same street. I never saw anybody stop to take pictures of the gentle-giant. It was as though there is enough room for everyone and everything that stood on this land called India. The tolerance that one can notice here even today is a legacy this nation had inherited over centuries old traditions and culture that has taught its people to be so. No wonder a man from this nation had to rise and prove that to the whole world.

"When I visited Ajmer, I realised the reverence people had towards saints, no matter which religion or faith they followed. My visit to Ajmer shrine of Sufi saint Chisti helped me experience this fact first hand. On whole I visited, rather followed the path Babajan had taken when she had come to India. I wanted to see what she must have felt when she must have visited India for the first time.

"All that I saw and all that I realised, India was a blend of people, traditions, ancient monuments standing next to modern ones, colourful representation of deities, fragrance of incense, traditional perfumes, flowers knitted in a garland or to be adorned by a beautiful young girl, roadside shacks that gave out a whiff of aroma that could mesmerise anyone to walk to it with your eyes closed, and the openhearted welcome the shack owner offered to anybody who visited. A guest in India, is considered to be equivalent to God, thus the over enthusiasm one can feel while being welcomed at a *dhaba* or the best five star hotels if one fancied. If any of those elements were to be separated, India would not be the same.

"Filth and poverty seemed noticeable, but it was less worrisome and horrific compared to the filth I had experienced in the impoverished minds of those various people who had come and gone in my life so far. At least these people could still be seen laughing and enjoying their moments as compared to those who had everything they could desire, and yet their faces wore a depressed expression. India was not one of the richest nations, but I found it to be a happy one, with its people still trying to find joy in little things of life and leaving what was beyond them to those who were beyond them. Every town, each village, and its people had a distinctive essence of its own. It was as if thousands and thousands of such little villages and towns had come together to form a nation called India. That was when I understood, why Indians living in London longed for their loved ones back home to visit them or why they appeared a bit incomplete even when they had earned the entire splendour one could afford.

"Wherever I went, I dropped a postcard to Lord Andrew and Dr Whitmore. Ten days later when I called up Lord Andrew, he wondered if I had given up my plans of studying as he was getting used to the idea of receiving a postcard from me almost every day. Indeed, I was excited and there was so much to see. It took me a good three weeks before I felt tired, exhausted of travel. I still had ten days on hand before the university opened for the year. Thus, I thought it would be wise to come down to Poona and arrange my stay and other necessities in the mean time.

"Poona seemed like an ancient woman who was now waking up to modernity. After checking into a hotel, I visited Hazrat Babajan's shrine, in a way to take her blessings and to have her permission to exhume her life. The humble monument of the saint, who had the glory of an Emperor to her repute, lay in a small shrine under the same *Neem* tree where she had once spent a good twenty-five years of her life. The whole experience humbled me to no end. It was as if I was visiting the grave of one of my ancestors. In a way, it was a fact. She was a Pathan and belonged to the royal family of which my father was a branch. Why destinies have to repeat themselves, I wondered. Probably because we need to relearn all that we had forgotten with time, I thought to myself as I stepped out.

"Finding a place to stay was least of the difficulties to solve. When I visited the university for the first time, I met Adnan there. He did not work in the university, but had flair with foreign students. He was more of a tout only meant for foreign students. As he said, 'Madam if you get into that queue, you will remain in until evening and still not end up finishing your work. If you give five hundred rupees, I would complete your work and get you out of here in an hour.' That was the first time I experienced corruption at such a level and that too in places of education. A few other students told me that Adnan was right and I could trust him with my documents. Besides helping me in my official formalities, he seemed an enthusiastic and resourceful person, who understood the needs of foreign students, the problems they faced while interacting with locals and the need to know that they were safe. Adnan was well acquainted with other foreign students and looked after their needs for a price. He claimed to have been doing so more as social service than for profit. He said he was an antique dealer and that was where he earned his bread and butter from; as for helping students, it kept him in touch with the youth and the college atmosphere that he never seemed to tire of, even though he was well over thirty-five or so I felt.

"That same day Adnan showed me a few apartments and I finalised one. It was a one-bedroom apartment and had a pleasant view overlooking its balcony and windows. I was further satisfied with the place as it was a short walk from the university and in calm vicinity. This would also save me the everyday hassle of arguing with the rickshaw-drivers to charge by the tariff meter and not according to the colour of the passenger's skin.

"In less than a month in India, I had set up myself to commence my research and work on a thesis in absolute freedom. I informed Lord Andrew of my progress from time to time and he seemed very amazed with my finds. Dr Whitmore kept suggesting methods I could adopt to further my search on the saint. The deeper I dived into Babajan's life, more I strengthened my belief that religion should never have collaborated with commerce. The lure of materialism had curled around religion like a venomous serpent that would never let go off his bind now.

"Various faiths had taught man a manner to conduct his life and respect the existence of others but materialism had gained over faith in time. Let's say materialism had found a new garb called faith, hiding beneath it has today managed to turn into faith itself. Even though humanity had battled innumerable wars under the pretext of guarding one faith or another, it was never devoid of the prospective territory, wealth and status as the real motives that man wished to possess or acquire.

Edward and his family were victims of this reality too. One could not conveniently ignore this unfortunate reality. When I immersed myself in my studies, I dwelled in a world that was devoid of the stark realities of uncivilised ways of today, where morality is up for auction, integrity has long been the serving slave of the power-lords, and insecurity reigned all over, like a queen.

"In comparison to all this, I was learning about a woman who had lived under a tree with tattered clothes on herself as her only belongings besides a few rings that she wore, until with age her fingers swelled, and the noble metal of the rings cut into her flesh. To such people, pain does not cause discomfort, I realised. Babajan had a steady followership, who insisted that she should be treated by a doctor when maggots began to fall out of her wounded fingers. She chose to let the maggots thrive on her flesh and lost two of her fingers in order to feed maggots.

"Intriguing as it may sound but anything living was to be valued and given an opportunity to exist, because only the worthy survives in the end, therefore there was no reason for us to grant ourselves the right to kill. We could protect ourselves from peril if we wished, but not turn offensive. Babajan spent her last twenty-five years in India when it was under British rule. Even those British officers seemed wondrous and concerned for the grand old *fakir,* who lived without a grudge under a tree, be it rain, sun or the winter chill. They too tried to build a place for her close to her tree, but she refused and remained there until her last breath, spreading love and compassion to whoever came her way.

"She was born a princess and died an empress in true sense, I thought. She had no boundaries to guard, no battles were ever needed to be fought and no palaces to be made to hold court. Under that *Neem* tree, she sat and her followers were her courtiers who would assemble in the court of her majesty and seek solutions to their innumerable problems, the kingdom of humanity was faced with in her times.

"She ruled unchallenged from her seat for she had realised that true power and might did not rest in the armouries of valiant armies or the treasuries of the kings. True power rested in a simple thought that we were allotted a lifetime to spread love, care and be of use to one another. Babajan had conquered her world that ways and would despise those who worried or wept over a menial loss in business or the desire to make more profits depriving someone else of his due.

"Every evening, when I would sit down to write, I would wonder that for centuries, people such as Hazrat Babajan had detected the root cause of troubles that humanity was faced with and had also prescribed the solutions to it. Unfortunately, why haven't we woken up to practise them? Such luminous souls have visited our planet from time and place-to-place, they have worked like satellites that spread the light of wisdom amongst humanity for centuries together, even though we do take pride that they existed, somehow and for some reason the light that beamed through them has not managed to affect all equally. We still choose to block those divine rays, for we hide ourselves behind thick, dark, smoky cloud cover of our wanton desires.

"The only consolation in such a scenario would be to understand that all such saints, seers, and thinkers knew where the world was heading and yet they chose to go about their task relentlessly. Their faith in the task they did has resulted in immortality of their thoughts and many like me still find a reason to come and seek their teachings, peer into their lives and understand the secrets of happiness that they had in plenty, without a dime in their pockets, they still considered themselves no less than the rulers of the universe."

❑❑❑

25

In the Circus of Life

"As my academic research gathered momentum, time had once again freed me from its bind. Meeting various people, whose parents had spent time with Babajan and interviewing those who remembered Babajan as a childhood memory, many were alive and remembered the grand old lady to be their doting grandmother, who would share a lot of stories of lands she had visited and times she had been through.

"Almost every day, I would schedule to meet someone, who was in some way associated with Babajan. Every interview resulted in a revelation of sorts. My task was not limited to feeling enamoured with my finds, but it was necessary to validate its authenticity and make a note of my observations on the same.

"A year had gone by and I was gearing up to begin serious writing based on my finds, when one day I received a shocking phone call from Lord Andrew. MI5 had arrested Dr Whitmore for having ties with the CIA for over two decades. The nature of his liaison was not clear, but in any case, no nation would tolerate a traitor. It was a jolt to me when I heard those words. Later that night, I recollected my discussion with him at his home and wondered why he had spend long years in the US soon after graduating with my father.

"Probabilities were plentiful, unfortunately; reality seemed unchangeable. My mentor was imprisoned for treason. Reality indeed was two-faced. On one side, Dr Whitmore remained a true friend to my father, while on the other side he had chosen to deceive the trust of the nation he belonged to. 'Nationalism is synonymous to hypocrisy,' he would often quote. Dr Whitmore staunchly believed that we were nobody to bind people into unseen boundaries and draw imaginary lines on the earth that would prescribe limits of how far one could go and which flag one would lay down his life for, if it came to that. When he spoke this way, it seemed an intriguing thought, but that day when his words echoed in my mind, I realised that he must have been chasing a dream that would never turn into a reality.

"I was saddened by the fact that I would never ever meet my mentor again. He had plans for me; he had things in his mind that he would say that he would tell when the time comes.

Who knew what he wanted to say and how he would do it now. Lord Andrew seemed concerned as he was very close to Dr Whitmore and wondered if the spooks were keeping a watch on him too. The only relieving news that came from London was that Edward had arrived at an arrangement with Claire and had decided to move to Los Angeles. They were living together, while three companies owned by Claire's father had filed bankruptcy and Claire's father himself had been arrested for misappropriation of funds. When one gets to hear about somebody being meted with justice, it strengthens your belief further in a simple phrase – 'One shall reap as one sows'.

"I was learning about the world where Babajan lived, that was two centuries ago while I was living in the present world today, which did not seem to be very different, but for a fact that the insecurity of the mighty few had not yet stooped to its rock-bottom in those times, to such an extent that even the common man was not spared. Today no one seems to have escaped the vicious sight of insecurity. She had indeed ruled long, well and intelligently in order to expand her empire that had not spared the rarest alleys where human life existed today.

"As though Dr Whitmore's arrest was not a shock enough, fate had more to offer in the form of a letter from Lord Andrew's secretary, a few months later. Lord Andrew had suffered a stroke that had left him paralysed in his right side with a blood clot in the brain that had resulted in his memory fading away rapidly. This resulted in a tremendous loss on the emotional level and an unthinkable one on the financial plane to me.

"Edward was inaccessible and so was the case with Lady Elizabeth. I could well imagine what that poor woman would have to deal with in such circumstances, an ailing husband on one hand, and an estranged son on the other. Lord Andrew's secretary was not permitted to remit money into my account until someone from the family instructed him to do so. Now that my only channel of communication, Lord Andrew himself was inaccessible, there was no way to get in touch with the family. The only option left was writing to Lady Elizabeth. I wrote a few times only to receive nothing from the other end.

"Fate, I thought, had once again found a new trap for me. My performance in the circus of life was similar to that of a trapeze artist. Just like he is tossed from one to another, fate has kept tossing me around from here to there; fortunately the grip of my mentors and mine over them had kept me from falling so far, but I wondered who would be the next one. Once again, I felt stranded. I did not know where I was to go, whom I could depend upon, and what I was to do after the completion of my thesis. I could survive a few months on my savings but I still had a long way to go.

"It was at that time when Adnan Peerzadeh stepped into my life once again. I shared my newfound financial concerns with him, as I knew he would not be interested in any of the rest and I did not feel the need for it, anyways. First thing he did, was to shift me to another place where I would have to share the apartment with a few other students. I did not mind that as long as it helped me save some more money. Next, he talked me into a part-time job at his warehouse. This also seemed like a welcome proposition. I was supposed to deliver very expensive and antiquated jewellery, charms, trinkets, and curios to the elite who ordered those. As he put it, he needed someone with a pleasing personality to do the job and my linguistic skills would add up to make me a suitable candidate for it. I could expect a salary that could pay off the balance fees I owed to the university.

"Once again, life had shaken me shortly and then set me calm. This time though, calm proved to be a short-lived one, as in the next few months, I was shuttled from one house to another three times and the present one was the fourth that I had come to stay in two months ago. At first, I shared an apartment with two other girls. Later, I moved in with a live-in couple, after which, I shared a sprawling apartment, that was already shared by two boys and their girlfriends. Most of the time they slept through the day as they worked the graveyard shift in some BPO and I managed to find the peace for I needed to concentrate on my thesis.

"I had no other option but to tolerate and adapt to whatever I could afford.

"Evenings were mostly spent visiting Adnan's clients in plush hotels or swanky pubs and restaurants. After working with him for a while, I asked him a few times of what exactly was I expected to do, for I felt I was doing nothing more than providing courier service. He would laugh and dismiss my questions and remind me that I was chasing a bigger goal

– PhD and that too on advent and need of religion. He would add that if the world would ever get to know more about a celestial soul such as Hazrat Babajan, it would be due to the efforts of people like myself. He would advise me that I should not deviate from the sole objective and let other things pass with time. After a few attempts, I stopped asking and we went about our lives the way we had been for a past few months.

"Finally, I had managed to complete my thesis and submit it well in time. I was awaiting my viva and I was worried of my future, as I had not heard from Lord Andrew's office in the past few months. Whenever I called his office his secretary would say that, 'He is better than before, but still needs rest.' What next, was the question that had captivated my total attention. I had nurtured myself to life once again due to Edward's insistence. After he walked away with a suitable bargain, academics took over my future with custodians like Dr Whitmore and Lord Andrew guarding my wellbeing.

"Now, one was behind the bars and the other was bound by clinical compulsions. With my earlier hopes laid to rest, I found myself in a precarious situation. I mean, I had nothing to prove my true nationality, as I possessed a Saudi passport even though I hailed from Afghanistan. Secondly, I could not return to London just like that, without a sponsor to back me, or a job that I could find well in time before I turned an illegal immigrant here, in India.

"So far my faith in my work and my efforts had rewarded me with a life unimaginable to anybody, but I feared if it was coming to an end as I could not even sight a mirage of hope that I could ask myself to walk to. I felt I had arrived into the final act in the circus of life. The acrobats that performed in a circus would take their chances from time to time, as they were aware of the safety net spread below. If they attempted an ingenious manoeuvre and failed, they would fall on the net and toss themselves up again. Even if the acrobats failed in their attempt, audience would applaud them for they tried.

"On the contrary, in the circus of life, neither there was a net to toss one back repeatedly nor there were many people to applaud one's genuine attempt, if one failed. If one miscalculated his act, then he would perish. Performing in the circus of life was a ruthless act and each one of us has had our fair share of wounds and scars. As long as we remain, we perform because we desire to be applauded and we take our chances to plan the most unthinkable manoeuvres. Many whom we look up to had succeeded in the past and we choose to forget those who hit the hard ground below. For apparent reasons, I was reminded of the fatal fall my father had succumbed to. Was it going to be my turn, I began to wonder."

❑❑❑

26

The Unfortunate Champ

"I would spend my days with this very thought looming over me until I became friends with a young woman in my neighbourhood. Her name was Shalini. She was married a few years ago and just like me had a lot of time on hand and very little to do as a homemaker. Since we lived a floor apart, we would meet regularly, go shopping together, and a few times went for movies too. Shalini's husband had very unpredictable working hours; therefore, she did not depend on him to take her out for such things.

"After a few weeks of bonding, I shared my realities with her. I also took her to Babajan's shrine. She was shocked to learn that Babajan had such an interesting life, after all, for a female to accomplish so much in those times, was nothing less than being termed commendable. As much as she was enamoured by my studies, she detested me for living in the atmosphere Adnan had put me in. I was sharing a three bedroom apartment with almost fourteen men, women and children, all put together, including myself.

"I would answer Shalini that with limited resources I had, this was the best I could afford; besides how else I would have found a friend like her? She would dismiss my reply with a smile and warn me that she instinctually did not feel good about Adnan. She knew that I was working for him and still she would insist that I should give it up. How was I going to do that, until I had an alternative in sight?

"My life had eventually resulted in a big zero, I would keep telling myself; and on one such evening, you arrived knocking my door. At least you have managed to rid me of all my contemplations. Now I know that I am heading towards a definite end for sure. I have told you everything without hiding away any facts. I wish that you should oblige me with an equally honest answer to the only question I have left."

I had to shake myself out of the trance-like silence I had slipped into, listening to Rosha.

"Yes why not?" I mumbled, clearing my throat. "I would definitely tell you all that I can," I replied reassuringly.

She peered into my eyes as if to check if I was truly going to answer her question or the officer within me would take over.

"Why are we being deported? I, for that matter, have a visa that permits me to live here for another two months. Please, at least tell me my offence."

I wondered what I could reply to that, for I was not investigating that case and I had just stepped in at the last moment when they were all to be evacuated. This kind of shuffling happens often in our line of work, but it could seem unbelievable to a common person. I said the same to Roṣha and she was disappointed with the answer. I did not expect any reaction other than that.

"Rosha, I have never ever overstepped in my line of duty, but believe me, I have no information other than the fact that you'll had been evading deportation for the past seven months and this time our men had the deportation orders prepared well in advance, therefore we raided the house and here you are now. Personally, I do not think you needed to be a part of all this, but then there must be a reason for it. If I knew it, I would have definitely told you."

She might have noticed the solemn sincerity in my eyes and said, "Probably you are speaking the truth, officer. But what a shame it is that I don't even know the crime I am being punished for."

Her eyes welled up as she turned to open the bag she was carrying with her. She drew a soft velvet pouch out of it and handed it over to me.

"Rosha, what is this?" I questioned before accepting it.

"Officer, I think you are the last sincere person I am going to meet here onwards, therefore keep it, before it ends up in some wrong hands. There are rose seeds in it."

"Rose seeds?" I questioned her curiously, as I dug into the bag and dropped a few on my palm to check. "I mean,

I have never heard of them, roses are usually planted from sliced stems."

"From where do you think the first stem originated from, officer?"

"I had not pursued biology or botany as a major, but had studied it compulsively in the course of my school days. Not once had this fact occurred to me that roses too would produce seeds even though they depended more on pollination for their spread," I said.

"My father had this hobby of harvesting rose seeds from the roses that blossomed in our garden. He had learnt this art from his father, and he, from his. That pouch is well over four generations old and some seeds too must be the same age. I wonder if those would germinate at all now," said Rosha and turned silent, preventing her tears from rolling onto her cheeks.

"Why are you giving me all of them, I could keep a few if you wish," I said to her.

"What am I to do with the rest? I used as many as I had to and I don't see a possibility of sowing them anymore, anywhere," replied Rosha.

Once again, it seemed like she was drawing herself into the shell that I had found her in at the beginning.

Teardrops swelled and balanced delicately on the tip of her eyes once again as she spoke, "I planted a few at my master's house in Saudi Arabia. Lord Andrew's garden grew even more fragrant when roses blossomed out of the seeds I had given to him. I had given enough to Zeba before leaving Kabul, and now I think the rest have to be given to someone from this country that has given me so much in the past two years. I would have wished to give a few to Shalini, had I left the usual way, but now I don't see how that is going to happen."

"Don't worry Rosha; I will have them sent to her. You can trust me for that at least. I also wish to tell you that you have travelled so far in your life, encountered such grave situations, that I am sure something good is in store for you."

Rosha shifted her gaze to me and said, "Isn't that hope that we all live with? But try putting the same question to a person who can see death waiting in front of him, and he will tell you how much more he wanted to do or how much more he could have accomplished if he had time on his hand. Somewhat similar is my case now onwards, officer."

"I am not trying to console you, Rosha. I am only following the frequency of chance you have had so far and going by its statistics, you stand a great chance of survival and even success."

"Officer, chance is like a lease that cannot be renewed endlessly, for ever. It has an end to it like all other things that exist, one day even chance ceases to exist in one's life."

What could I tell her further? How could I console someone like Rosha, who knew that she had done all that she needed to come out a winner, but for some ruthlessly biased judges who decided against granting her the title. Only if I had known her a few days earlier and only if she had told me all that she told me then, I could have pulled her out of the mess she was into.

I mean how much a person really needs to live? Food, clothing, and shelter; I could have happily provided her with all that and for the rest we could have come out with some solution in the time being.

My wife and children would have welcomed her, I would have found a younger sister that I never had, and Rosha would have found a family that she did not have. Fortunately, my wife and I were not the ones who sternly believed in blood relations alone. For us she would have been like another family member, whose responsibility I would gladly accept to take. However, that 'only if' had not been the case this time. My resentment, my solutions, my helplessness, all was mounting over me at the same time and I was bound by duty that prevented me from voicing any of it to Rosha. Just like many other secrets that remained locked in our hearts, this one too would have to end up in the dark, airless cellar.

❑❑❑

27

On a Wing and a Prayer

As if I had turned a better thinker than Rosha, I kept reasoning with her, and the moment, which I was trying to evade in all my banter arrived echoing loud and clear from the overhead speakers. The flight Rosha was going to travel in was ready for boarding. The decisive moment had arrived. I felt like a jail superintendant who had walked an innocent to the gallows already and now it was time to pull the lever and walk away with the guilt of reality, which only he would remain privy to.

Somewhere deep down even I knew that Rosha had slim to none possibilities of any aid in the country she was being deported to. I had to escort her into the aircraft before any passengers could board. I walked her to the aircraft with a mixed bag of feelings, similar to the bag of rose seeds she had given me. Just as none of them would blossom into the same specie, my feelings were variant too. For once, I felt like a brother who was as if bidding his newly-wed sister farewell. Another moment I felt like walking the innocent who was condemned to death. I felt like helping her escape. All those emotions and many more stormed my mind one after the other as I escorted her through the aerobridge to the gate of the aircraft. I flashed my ID to the airhostess and we found our way to Rosha's seat.

The end had arrived at last, indeed. Separation was irreversible from here on. Trying as much as I could to maintain my composure, I could not stop myself from hugging her. Rosha responded with equal warmth and I slipped a piece of paper with my telephone numbers and email address to her.

"Write to me that you are safe," I uttered to her with great difficulty and control over my choking voice.

She asked, "What can I consider you to be, officer, that I should write to you?"

"A friend, an elder brother, or anything else that may please you, besides a husband as I… am married and you deserve a better suitor," I replied flashing my ring finger at her.

We managed to smile at each other in that moment of remorse. I knew myself too well to be sure that if I stayed there any longer, I would lose hold over myself. Therefore, I waved my hand over Rosha's head like a blessing, pushed her gently into her seat, put the seat belt on for her and did all to evade our eyes from meeting again. But, how much was left to do anyways?

"Goodbye officer," said Rosha in her gentle and calm tone. I just managed to stand straight, look into her eyes and her face that wore a saintly smile; words and voice had failed me altogether at that moment. With that image of Rosha embedded in my mind, I walked out of the aircraft, out of the aerobridge and out of the airport.

I wiped my own brimming tears off my eyes as I lit a cigarette and kept gazing at the beautifully lit runway. Rosha's aircraft too was going to take off from the same runway 9-27. I smoked and waited to get the last view of the aircraft taking off.

For some unknown reason, I always fill with hope at the sight of an aircraft taking off. A mammoth machine that charges its way battling through the opposite winds and lifts off, escaping, disappearing into the clouds. No matter how many times I have witnessed this phenomenon, I have not tired myself of a repeat.

One of my colleagues called me on my cell. I told them that they could leave as I had decided to rest at a relative's house before returning. They headed back home and I waited for Rosha's plane to roll.

Soon enough the gigantic 747 began to taxi towards the runway in front of my eyes. My heart pounded with fear as the engines of the jumbo rumbled with the increasing throttle. While the aircraft moved further and away, my heartbeat gathered pace. I just could not understand what I was fearful of and why. I was experienced enough to handle such situations, but then something within me reminded me that this experience was not the usual one. It was rare, indeed it was, but the dilemma was that I had unfortunately overstepped the line and had begun to feel concerned for Rosha.

She was not a criminal that deserved such a stern punishment. Finally, as for our responsibilities and duties and that of our nation, we had done what was required, but as for my sentiments in this case, that were not bound by nation or my duty alone, needed more time to come to terms.

A few minutes later, the mighty 747 thundered down the runway at colossal speed and lifted off with a deportee seated in it that I was never going to forget. I kept looking at the strobes of that aircraft until I could see it no more. Once again, the sun had turned the sky scarlet, signalling its arrival. Rosha's journeys had always coincided with the rising and the setting sun. But this one worried me as she was returning to the same hell she had once left for good.

❑❑❑

28

Fresh Wounds & Time Balm

I hailed a taxi to the intercity bus stand. As I rested myself in it, the driver asked me if he could play some music. I consented and he switched the radio on. As if I was not disturbed enough with the happenings of the night gone by, the song was going to provide fuel to fire.

"Jaane Kahaan Gaye Woh Din, Kehte The Teri Rah Mein Nazron Ko Hum Bichayenge" (Wonder where have those days disappeared when my eyes would long for a glimpse of you). A befitting song for that moment brought forth the visuals of Raj Kapoor dressed as a puppet clown, tangled in a web of strings symbolising his helplessness.

The visuals of that song were not very different from the visuals my own eyes had witnessed few moments ago. No wonder Raj Kapoor is considered an incomparable master of his craft I thought. He had visualised the emotion of helplessness and separation over thirty years ago, and immortalised it on celluloid, while I was to experience it first-hand that day.

Mera Naam Joker is one of my all time favourite films. I saw a lot of me in it. The situation of this song had spared me so far, now that too had sneaked into my life as an addition to the list of my experiences. The song lingered in my ears until I reached home, showered, and tried to rest in the laps of sleep for a few hours.

A few days passed in usual routine at office. Colleagues knew that I was disturbed; therefore, they intentionally never brought up a mention to that fateful deportation raid. I had deposited the pouch that Rosha had given me, into the drawer of my table. A few of my colleagues had seen me take it from her at the airport and a few others had seen it when I brought it to the office.

Soon I got busy with new operations and so did others, and Rosha began to fade away from my immediate memory. But whenever I returned home in time and poured myself a drink, the thought of Rosha would spread in my mind, just as whisky blends into one's blood stream with the first sip one takes. Fortunately, there weren't many such occasions, thus I was able to keep myself from being reminded of her often.

Life does have its own mysterious ways of providing you with the strength to overcome unfortunate moments, and live for those that still exist and for those tasks that still await completion. One has to let go of certain unfortunate fatalities in life and move on, rather than sit and ponder over things that were never in our control. I was doing the same and hoped that Rosha was too.

❑❑❑

29

Autopsy of Virtue

Life returned to its absolute usual self and I was the same ruthless officer to the guilty once again, until one day, almost two months later, when I received an email in my personal mail account. The sender seemed nobody I knew or in my address list. I ran a spam check and opened to read it. Rosha had written to me!

Dear Vishal,

If I am permitted to address you like this or respected officer, which suits you better. I have been staying at this detention centre ever since I landed here. Authorities have been working on my deportation to Kabul.

The intensive efforts that the authorities are putting into my case, it seems likely that they would successfully manage to deport me to my home in Kabul. On reaching there, I am sure I will be received by an impatient mob of murderers who have done my family to dust.

At least I am now surer of one fact, that they would bury me in my courtyard. I hope Zeba is still alive to sow some rose seeds on my grave.

I am writing to you with a request, as I have timed this mail to reach you only after forty days. If this mail reaches you faster than my voice over a phone call, assume that your Rosha has finally blended into dust.

Therefore the request – kindly perform my fortieth day at the Babajan Shrine. I am sorry to put you through this trouble, but you are the last available relation I have.

With love

Rosha

My wife had once called me overseas to give me the news of my maternal grandmother's demise. Even though she was my grandmother for namesake, in reality she was the one who had mothered me from the time I was born. I did not shudder as much even then as I did when I read this email from Rosha. My grandmother passed away at a ripe age of eighty-four. She had seen me grow, get married and had spent time with my children too. In short, she had lived a wholesome life. But in Rosha's case, she was just about to begin, and dead already? A harsh fact to digest, I corresponded with our counterpart in Kabul with details of Rosha.

Forty-eight hours later, I received a confirmation of the tragic reality in the form of an internal communication. A girl matching the description I had shared had indeed been disrobed and paraded to an erstwhile football field in Kabul, and then shot in the head once from a .44 calibre revolver. Her body was left there for the hawks and vultures to feast on, when an old woman claimed it and offered burial. That old woman, I assumed must have been Zeba and she would have arranged to bury Rosha alongside her family in the courtyard of her very own house.

It reminded me of her words, 'Duality of Reality'. Two aspects of the same fact, one grieved me no end that some insecure and prejudiced guardians of faith had terminated a life that could have proved a boon to plenty and the other gave me solace that finally she had united with her family. If not in this world, then wherever one went to after death. In any case, our world had no room left for idealists and virtuous people who valued human existence over everything else, like Rosha's family. We had learnt well in time to speak one thing and do the exact opposite. Now the problem I was faced with was – how was I going to come to terms with myself?

My immediate reaction after that was to walk up to one of my colleagues and ask him out for a smoke. He obliged and we were off to a *paan* shop. Some minister, I thought, needed to realise that his adamant ban on smoking in offices and public places was no way going to stop one from smoking. Indeed smoking is injurious to health, but then what about the bigger hazards that surround our lives today? I was angry, and shrapnel of my angst began to fly in every direction.

As I lit the cigarette of my colleague, I reminded him of that fateful deportation case. He was slightly surprised for I had enquired about it after so many days. Anyways, what he revealed was that Adnan Peerzadeh was on his radar of attention for long and for various reasons. Adnan was into drug trafficking, gunrunning, prostitution, and money laundering. I wondered how Rosha had surfaced in this mess. My colleague revealed that Adnan disguised packets of Cocaine and Marijuana in those boxes and souvenirs that Rosha helped deliver to his clients. To my colleague, she was a part of this little cartel. I would have thought so too, if I were working on that case. Adnan had over two hundred thousand USD in his bank accounts in India and was currently cooling his heels in judicial custody.

In short, Rosha had resulted into a victim of circumstance. Her knowledge of how the world should have been did not spare her the sight to realise which trap she was walking into when she accepted to work for Adnan. It was plain unfortunate. It angered me to no end, but what was I going to do? A few puffs later, I asked my colleague where he had found his leads. He knew that I would not go that far without a reason. He revealed that Adnan's operatives had come to stay in the same building as one of our junior colleagues.

"Is his wife's name Shalini?" I asked almost immediately. My colleagues jaw dropped with surprise. I had found my answer. I walked away in silence and without any reaction.

As we walked back to the office, I thought to myself, should I commend the wife of a fellow officer for what information she had shared with her husband about Rosha? Or should I let her know that her friend who had desired to gift her some rose seeds was murdered and was now six feet below the sea level, all because she might have been a wee bit over-enthusiastic in revealing her finds to her husband?

I dismissed all those speculations, as it was a futile case study as of now. I had to fulfil Rosha's request and honour the struggles of an unfortunate princess.

❑❑❑

30

"Alvida Princess!"

Next morning I bathed and readied myself for work like any other day. Everyone at home thought it was routine. Instead of the office, I drove to a flower vendor in the neighbourhood of Hazrat Babajan's shrine. I ordered him to make a *chaddar* (sheet) of fresh red roses to be spread over Babajan's tomb. The flower vendor's temper kept rising as I interfered and sifted the fresh red roses from the wrinkled ones. Price was not the issue that day, and I was not bothered of the cost.

After all a princess had died, how could I spread a wreath of soiled flowers on her remains? A person, who had turned so dear to me in the shortest time, had passed away, and had left me with the responsibility of fulfilling her dying wish; how was I to think of the financial dent when the emotional dent had resulted in an unthinkable loss?

I did not know the ways or formalities to be carried out at the shrine; in any case, as I approached it with the *chaddar,* I realised I was too late for that. Someone noticed the flowers in my hand and walked towards me to take it. I followed him into the shrine and helped him spread it all over the saint's grave that Rosha had fallen in love with. While he chanted some couplets from the Holy Quran, I kept gazing at the tomb, as if I had spread a sheet of roses on Rosha's grave.

Strange are the ways of the world I thought to myself. A princess had her ways of thanking another in life and even after death. Hazrat Babajan too was a princess and her legacy prevailed even after her death in 1932. The princess that came to learn about Babajan had been showered with gifts of virtues that she could take back with her. Unfortunately, life did not give her an opportunity to thank the elder princess herself and I stood there for Rosha as her emissary in the court of Empress Babajan.

I don't remember how long I stood there. I don't know how many others came and left. I stepped out of that place when sun was brimming hot and signalled afternoon. How many people have that effect on others in today's times, I wonder. How many people are capable to do so in a few hours, is beyond my comprehension.

That day I chose to escape all responsibilities and retire to a place where I could ponder over all that had gone by. That is what I did. I had discovered an ocean of thoughts that gave rise to waves, which soared and lashed the shores of my ethos.

Thoughts that demanded answers, some of which were hard to find... some I knew but was ashamed to reveal, many that all of us need to think about and act before each one of us would soon have to turn into a silent spectator and witness executions of many more like Rosha....

What have we turned ourselves into with all the advancement, evolution and science put together? Nothing more than another kind of machine that is capable to think of its survival before anything and anybody else. If that is all we wished to become, then why were we conferred a brain that could think beyond anyone else in the animal kingdom?

If we were marching towards a day when we would hunt our own kind, not for survival but for prejudice, were all the discoveries necessary or worthwhile? Were the discoverers or thinkers of the yore expecting this result of their toils?

Morality, too was considered a science, I remember having attended periods of the same throughout my school days. Then why all of a sudden did we decide to learn it and never practise it in day-to-day life?

How much wealth could make a man say – Enough! How far does one aim to rule and how would he watch upon his complete empire in one glance? No conqueror had come close to turn that dream into reality and no one shall in time to come.

Even then, man is mesmerised to grab as much as he can. Like a glutton, he alone wishes to relish the feast called life on this earth. Have we forgotten that ultimately we do not possess the right to choose our final resting place? What if the king and his opponent were buried in neighbouring graves? The dead lose all that is earthly valued. How many funerals does one need to attend in order to understand the fact of life? Ultimately, one day, death shall bind herself around us, and take us to a different plane altogether. I am sure, with the result of our doings here, we would be the most cursed animals of that next plane.

But why should we bother about all that today, while breath is still loyal to us and we have not fared that badly on our ethical quotient? Silence and ignorance are what most of us have pledged our loyalty to. So wait until each one realises that we have waited too long, and now it is our turn to roll into the pit. All our achievements, balance sheets, ownerships of endless hectares of land would one day transform all of us to dust. Wait until that day when the mighty alive would be reduced to a helpless dead; with his eyes open, he would create an illusion that he is still breathing until one would throw that very same earth on his face that he had battled for all his life.

Questions, questions and more questions kept slapping me continuously until I arrived back home. Nobody knew where I had been and no one enquired. They knew my nature of work and I was not in one of my best moods that night. My wife asked me if I was going to have dinner; I refused. She gauged that I was at home but my mind was elsewhere.

That night she drew close to me and asked me what was bothering me, when she noticed my eyes were wide open, staring into the darkness of night, with my tears glistening in the rays of the moonlight that pierced its way through our bedroom window. Tears and I were a rare combination and my wife had not witnessed that in fifteen years of our marriage.

"What happened, why are you crying?" she asked worriedly.

I replied, "A princess had died."

I know my reply to her was bizarre, but I could say no more. She did not probe further and let me be. I don't remember how sleep gathered me in her bind and how long I slept for. But I very clearly remember that I had no dreams or nightmares that night.

❑❑❑

31

Rosha Returns

A day later, I returned home with a beautiful pot filled with manure-laden earth and a few seeds from Rosha's pouch. My children and my wife wondered as I placed that beautiful pot on the table. It wasn't an urn of Rosha's ashes, rather it contained her spirit in it, I felt, as I drew my children closer and explained to them how they were supposed to look after it.

That night I thought to myself, that I had a true wish to help Rosha and if that demanded keeping her in my place, then I was ready for that too. I had genuinely desired to look after her and in a way she had agreed to my requests and had come home. Now whether we proved to be worthy hosts or not, remained to be seen.

My son watered the pot as my daughter wondered why. A few days or probably a week later, my children were delighted to notice sprouts in the pot. The rose seeds had germinated. Then the first bud formed, and a few days later, it bloomed into a fragrant rose.

My daughter seemed enamoured by its fragrance and wished to pluck it to show-off to her schoolmates. My son smiled in relief that the plant had finally accomplished its task; to my wife it was a rose that she had never seen before, and the fragrance she had never smelt. As for me, a whiff of that fragrance and the size of the blossoming of that flower symbolised the large-heartedness of Rosha. I was relieved of my worries. Rosha had finally communicated that she liked our company and care, thus that blossoming rose seemed like a symbol of gratitude from her side to all of us.

Rosha had achieved immortality by sowing those seeds of roses in the land that gave her pain and then showed her a path to live. Rosha, just like her name, had spread blossoms of fragrance wherever she had stepped foot. I realised that she had immortalised as sweet fragrance, that was similar to a rose. She had found a way to live after death and across continents.

That day I was reminded of Shalini. As promised to Rosha, I went to her house and gave her a few seeds packed in a small gift-wrapped box. I wished that she plants them and nurtures them well. She was not aware of the fact that Rosha was no more. I did not think it was necessary to tell her the whole story.

Today our family has gotten used to Rosha's presence, and she cares for us with a fresh blossom every morning. That evening, the flower show granted Rosha the title that humanity had refused her all her life. For some reasons we haven't grown that ruthless and intolerable yet that we begin to check the nationalities of flowers too. Just like that, beautiful rose that had won that evening, Rosha was a person who could not have remained captive in the binds of one nation when she wanted to share herself with the whole world. In our physical world, Rosha could never have possibly lived to see such a day. However, in her death she found the way of fulfilling her desires. She blended into a beautiful flower that Nature could spread all over and the fragrance that could carry itself to distances with gentle breeze.

How could I have explained all this to the enthusiastic horticulturists, that we had reared our champion flower with the realisation of the fact that reminded us the importance of human life over everything else? How could anybody understand that we needed to understand that so many Roshas might have perished without an option to immortalise their trace? Just like the plant, we need to realise that human life and concern for each other was equally important, probably more important than all else. All we needed was to realise this fact and practise it diligently.

Only then, could we have the privilege to see Roshas flourish in flesh and blood. Only then, could we applaud their manoeuvres in the circus of life; and if they were to ever fall, we would respond with concern and place them at the right heights once again, so that they could try once again.

I know I am not qualified enough to write anything on behalf of Rosha. However, today I seem to be left with no option other than share all that I learnt in those few hours of her company. If this secret remains a secret within me for life, then I would consider myself a culprit equal to those who have plundered humanity for their own profits.

All that has gone by, needed a little more effort, time and integrity to bring forward a life that could have gone unnoticed – therefore this attempt of mine!

❑❑❑